A loud sound tore the night.

I lurched and fell against the car door. Straightening, I stared in disbelief at the small hole in my windshield and the cobwebby cracks that radiated from it.

I barely had time to register "shot" when Curt, gloves off and on his knees looking for my keys, grabbed the back of my coat and pulled me abruptly down.

A second shot fragmented the side window above our heads. Little pieces of glass rained down on us, stinging our faces and getting caught in our hair.

"Around the other side of the car," Curt ordered. "Hurry! We're too exposed here! And keep down."

"This isn't some accident, you know," I said. "It's got something to do with Patrick Marten."

"Who's Patrick Marten?" Curt asked.

"He's the dead man I found in my trunk last night."

Books by Gayle Roper

Love Inspired Suspense

See No Evil #39
Caught in the Middle #50

GAYLE ROPER

has always loved stories, and as a result she's authored 40 books. Gayle has won the Romance Writers of America's RITA® Award for Best Inspirational Romance, finaled repeatedly in both the RITA Award and the Christy® Award contests, won three Holt Medallions, the Reviewers' Choice Award, the Inspirational Readers Choice Contest and a Lifetime Achievement Award, as well as the Award of Excellence. Several writers' conferences have cited her for her contributions to the training of writers. Her articles have appeared in numerous periodicals including *Discipleship Journal* and *Moody Magazine,* and she has contributed chapters and short stories to several anthologies. She enjoys speaking at writers' conferences and women's events, reading and eating out. She adores her kids and grandkids, and loves her own personal patron of the arts, her husband, Chuck.

GAYLE ROPER

caught in the middle

Revised by author.

Steeple
Hill®

Published by Steeple Hill Books™

STEEPLE HILL BOOKS

Steeple
Hill®

ISBN-13: 978-0-373-44240-9
ISBN-10:   0-373-44240-8

CAUGHT IN THE MIDDLE

This is the revised text of the work which was first published by Zondervan in 1997.

www.SteepleHill.com

Printed in U.S.A.

I will instruct you and teach you in the way you should go; I will counsel you and watch over you.
—*Psalms* 32:8

For Georgia with great affection
I love your love for the Lord

ONE

"It was a dark and sleety night," I muttered as I slid behind the wheel and slammed the car door, grateful to have reached protection without drowning. I tossed my briefcase onto the seat and shook the water out of my short, spiky hair.

"Merrileigh Kramer, what have you done?" my mother had asked in horror when I'd had my waist-length hair drastically cut at summer's end on the new-look, new-person theory.

I looked in the mirror and wondered the same thing myself. I hadn't cut my hair, except for its annual split-ends trimming, since ninth grade. For a woman who hated change, I did a very drastic thing when I entered that beauty parlor. And it had only been step one.

Now I sighed and reminded myself that it'd grow eventually. The only trouble was that I didn't know what to do with it while it grew. Somehow women routinely got from Halle Berry short to Halle Berry long and looked good in the process. I feared there wasn't enough mousse in the world for me to accomplish that feat.

I eased my way across the parking lot, uncertain

how slippery the millions of needles of icy rain had made things. The others who had been attending the Wednesday evening Board of Education meeting with me moved just as slowly. What had begun as a cold, nasty rain had turned to sleet when we weren't looking.

When it was my turn to pull out onto the road, I stepped slowly on the gas. The wheels spun for an instant on the thin layer of ice, then grabbed hold.

I hated ice. Every time I drove on it, I thought of my mother and the winter's day in Pittsburgh years ago when she had been driving me and four friends home from Brownies. I remembered the terrifying spin across the other lane and the oncoming cars scrambling to avoid us. I remembered the thud of our car as it hit a utility pole. I still felt my heaving stomach and tasted the fear. Mostly I remembered the screams and my mother's white face and the blood from the bashed noses. The fact that no one had been badly hurt then did not ease my fluttery heart tonight.

I drove carefully, watching for trouble. At Manor Avenue and Lyme Street I detoured slowly around a pair of cars half blocking the intersection as they sat with their left headlights locked together. Their drivers stood in the rain doing a good imitation of their cars, noses mere inches apart.

I couldn't help grinning at them, but I gripped the wheel more tightly. My heart throbbed in my temple.

With relief I turned onto Main Street where traffic was moving more quickly, keeping the road from freezing. When I passed *The News* office, the lights were still on, and I felt a surge of belonging. I beeped my horn in greeting to whomever was working so late. Don, my fearsome editor? Mac, his lecherous but charming assistant? Larry, the sports guy?

Tomorrow Don would bestow upon me the honor of writing a story about the first ice storm of the season. I knew it. Such stories were favorite ploys of editors, and as new kid on the block, I was certain to get the assignment.

I'd had worse. At least there'd be plenty of material in the police report about all the fender benders. Between the ice storm and the Board of Education meeting, I'd be plenty busy before morning deadline. Then I had scheduled the interview with the local artist. Variety to be sure.

I turned onto Oak Lane and felt the wheels slew. *Hang on,* I told myself. *You're almost home.*

I took my foot off the gas, gritted my teeth and proceeded slowly between the rows of cars parked against each curb.

Suddenly a car on my right roared to life like a lion scenting its prey. Without looking, it sprang from its parking spot, barely leaving the paint on my fender. I instinctively did exactly what I'd always lectured myself about not doing. I hit the brakes hard on ice.

Of course I went into an immediate skid. My headlights raked across the offending car as it pulled away, briefly revealing a man, hat pulled down over his eyes, collar up against the weather, staring intently ahead, completely unaware of me or anything else.

My stomach became mush and my heart thumped wildly in my ears as I skidded helplessly toward a new blue car parked on the left. I whipped my wheel into the skid just like everyone said you should, but still the shiny blue door panels with their navy-and-red racing stripes rushed at me. My headlights blazed on the chrome; the black windows loomed darkly.

But my real terror was for the man who had suddenly materialized at the front bumper of the blue car, standing like a pedestrian waiting for a clear path to jaywalk. I had no idea where he'd come from.

"Please, God, don't let me hit him!" I was a Brownie again, panic-stricken.

His features were indistinct through my rain-washed window, but I could see the *O* of his mouth as he saw me rushing toward him. He turned to run.

I closed my eyes involuntarily against the crash, shoulders hunched, face screwed up in apprehension. I was probably screaming, but thankfully I don't remember. Screaming has always struck me as a sign of weakness, and I like to imagine that I react with style even when I'm afraid. And I was afraid.

After a very long, slow-motion moment, my car shuddered to a silent halt. I cautiously opened my eyes and found myself mere inches from the blue car's front fender, the two cars neatly side-by-side and too close together for my door to open. I could not have parked so well had I tried.

I slid across the seat and flung open the far door. I didn't think I'd hit the man—I had neither heard nor felt a thump—but I had to make sure he wasn't crushed beneath my wheels. I pressed a hand against my anxiety-cramped abdomen and climbed into the downpour.

The man wasn't lying broken on the road. In fact,

he wasn't anywhere, lying or standing, broken or whole. He had completely disappeared.

I leaned against my car, weak with relief, and took deep breaths. I barely felt the icy sleet running down my neck. Finally I was able to move enough to get myself back into the car and, with a strange, shaky feeling, I drove the few remaining blocks home. I couldn't wait to get there, take a hot shower and relax with Whiskers purring on my lap as I drank a Diet Coke and ate a handful of Oreos. By then my heart would probably be beating normally again.

My snug, cozy, carriage-house apartment had once been part of the estate of Amhearst's leading citizen, Charlie Mullens, a man who'd made millions in the stock market in the twenties and had built a great mansion to forget his New York tenement beginnings. He had lost his fortune in the Great Crash of '29 and his life shortly afterward when he drove the new Rolls-Royce he could no longer pay for into the railroad overpass. His heirs, reduced to working for a living, soon sold the gracious, money-eating mansion and moved from Amhearst.

Over the next forty years, the property passed from hand to hand, deteriorating steadily until it was razed in the early seventies. At that time the carriage house, which had sat peacefully behind the mansion unnoticed and unused, was renovated into four one-bedroom apartments, two on the ground floor, two above. A long, narrow drive off Oak Lane gave access to the quaint building, and I turned down the drive, grateful to be home.

It was still somewhat strange to me that this *was*

home. Here I was, all alone in Amhearst, working as a reporter at *The News,* responsible to no one but God and Don Eldredge, the newspaper's owner-editor.

I don't have to do anything, I had understood one evening during my first week in Amhearst. *I'm completely on my own. If I want to eat and pay the rent, I'd better go to work, but I don't have to. And there's no one here who cares enough to make me.*

It had been a strange, lonely and frightening realization. There were no family, no friends, no acquaintances here. It was just me, making my own choices. The next day I went to the animal shelter and got Whiskers, a huge gray-and-white mottled cat with marvelous white whiskers. Now at least I was responsible to one living being. Now I had to fulfill at least one obligation every day, or my shins would be black-and-blue from Whiskers butting them, his special way of asking for his dinner.

Leaving Pittsburgh and home had been hard for me. I like to think of myself as independent, but the truth is that I like to be "independent" surrounded by familiar things.

I'd gone back home after college, moving in with my parents, content to be where everything was known and comfortable. I hadn't had to find a new doctor or a new dentist or a new church. I'd become a general reporter at the paper where I had worked for three of my college summers, and I'd done very well, even winning a couple of minor journalism awards.

And, of course, Jack was in Pittsburgh: handsome, personable, accomplished, irresponsible Jack.

I had expected to live at home one, maybe two,

years at the very longest. After all, I was an independent spirit. I was amazed and appalled when I woke up one day and realized that I had been there four years, waiting for life to happen. Waiting for Jack.

"Just a little more time, Merry," he'd say. "That's all I'm asking. Just a little more time."

Eventually, to save myself from drowning in despair, I came to Amhearst, and my first weeks here were terrible. I hated all the new people, the new streets, the new stores. I got a toothache, probably from grinding my teeth all night in fear, and I had to find a dentist. I hated him, too.

But I made it. I learned to like my job, and I slowly remembered that being alone isn't the worst thing in the world. I might not be laughing much yet, but I was slowly regaining some self-respect.

"Forgetting what is behind," Dad said one night on the phone, quoting St. Paul. "Straining toward what is ahead. Pressing on toward a new life. We're proud of you, Merry."

Jack spoke to me on the phone a few times, too, and even came to visit me once. I agonized over that visit, filled with equal measures of hope and dread. The reality was dull compared to my nightmares and daydreams.

"Come back when you're ready to get married," he told me when he left.

"I'll come back when I have a ring on my finger and a date on the calendar, not before," I replied. Then I went into my apartment and cried myself sick.

And so summer became fall, and fall a nasty, sleety, early December night with icy roads, and I was finally home.

I parked, climbed out into the cold and wet, and hurried to my trunk, where I'd stashed a case of Diet Coke. The dim light by the walk barely illuminated the area.

I looked uncomfortably over my shoulder. It was dark and spooky back here even on a nice night, but in the rain and sleet, it was worse than usual. The large lilac at the edge of the house was especially eerie tonight, with its branches creaking and complaining about their icy bath.

I eyed the dripping tree, trying to penetrate it to be certain it wasn't hiding someone. Come May, those blossoms had better be beautiful and fragrant to make up for my heart palpitations the rest of the year.

Although, I told myself with false bravado, no bad guy in his right mind would be lurking behind a lilac tree on a night like this.

Even so, the last thing I expected to find when I raised the lid of my trunk was a dead body.

TWO

Instinctively I slammed the lid down. I stood, shocked, until a sudden, stout gust of wind made the lilac creak alarmingly. I jumped and swung around, but of course no one was there. We were alone, the corpse in my trunk and I.

It can't be true, I thought. *It simply can't be. Things like this don't happen to real people, just people in mystery novels. My mind is playing tricks on me because I'm tired and had such a nerve-racking trip home.*

I looked at the dark outline of my trunk lid. The slight illumination from the light by the walk glinted on my keys still dangling in the lock.

I raised the lid just far enough for the light to come on, then bent cautiously and peeked in.

There was a body, all right. A man. He had on a green, down-filled jacket, and he was lying on his stomach, his face turned away.

I slammed the lid again and made it to the porch just in time to sit before I fell. I put my head between my knees and stared blankly at the wet cement.

There was a body in my car!

When I could move again, I stumbled into my apartment and called the police.

"Please come quickly!" I hardly recognized my shaky voice. "Please."

I got out of my wet clothes and into my heaviest sweats. I toweled my hair and went to wait numbly at the front door, my breath frosting the glass of the storm sash.

When the first flashing light turned down the alley, I ran to the parking area. Soon I was standing under my gray umbrella surrounded by men in dripping, bright-orange slickers with POLICE written in black on their backs.

"First question," said one. "Did you touch anything?"

I shook my head, horrified at the thought.

"Okay, then," he said. "What happened?"

"I was going to get a case of sodas out of my trunk. I opened it and there was this body."

He looked at me, eyebrows raised, waiting for more. "That's it?"

I looked back, aghast. "A body isn't enough?"

He smiled. "Open the trunk for us, please."

Obediently, I did. "See?" I pointed helpfully at the corpse sprawled on top of a cardboard box filled with two dozen cans of decaf Diet Coke.

I swallowed convulsively and looked away. My stomach was teeming with acid, and my mouth tasted like metal. The flashing lights and the crackling car radios did nothing to ease my tension.

The policeman, a beefy man with a heavily seamed face, studied the body.

"Who is he?"

I stared at the policeman, thunderstruck. "How should I know?"

"It *is* your car," said the policeman reasonably.

"Well, it isn't my body!"

"Oh." The policeman's voice was neither believing nor disbelieving. "Then you've looked at him well enough to know you don't recognize him?"

I swallowed hard a couple of times against the thought of studying the man. "Are you kidding? I haven't gone near him. See me? I'm standing with my back to the car so I don't have to look at him."

"Then how do you know you don't know him?"

"I just know."

"Uh-huh. Well, why don't you tell me exactly what happened here tonight."

I had never felt so unreal in my life. My car was now bathed in bright light supplied by portable generators rumbling in a van with RESCUE in red-and-gold letters on its white side. Two policemen were trying to arrange a plastic tarp to shield the whole area from the weather. One tied some ropes to the creaky lilac, and the other hammered some pegs into the macadam of the parking area and looped ropes around them.

The vanity license plate my brother, Sam, had given me for my birthday mocked the intense scene. MERRY, it read.

"So you'll remember who you are, and so you'll remember to be happy," he said when he gave it to me. What he wasn't saying was that he wanted me to forget Jack, but I knew. I had looked at the plate, knowing the love and concern that went into his ordering it, knowing he couldn't have foretold that my romantic trials would force me to decide to move just when he planned to give it to me. But the truth was that MERRY was a heart-piercing reminder of the un-Merry person I had become.

Now my car, my trunk, my parking lot, even MERRY had become police business.

I sighed as I watched another heavy peg pounded into the macadam. Hopefully my landlord would understand that it was the police who had made the holes in his parking area, not me. Somehow, knowing Mr. Jacobs, I doubted it.

"Miss Kramer, please tell me what happened here tonight," the policeman repeated.

I forced my eyes from the activity and looked at him. "Nothing much happened here," I said. "I opened my trunk, and there he was. I closed my trunk, hoping he'd go away. I opened my trunk and he was still there. I called you."

"That's it?"

"That's it."

A car squealed into the alley behind the official cars. A man climbed out and walked authoritatively toward the open trunk. He leaned under the protective plastic and around the men taking photographs, studied the situation, then walked to the policeman and me.

As he watched the approaching man, the policeman snorted, little puffs of foggy breath erupting from each nostril. "The press already! That's all we need."

"Don!" I said as I flung myself at the man. He ducked to miss the points of my umbrella and patted me comfortingly on the back.

"It'll be okay," he said as though to a crying child. "It'll be okay."

Suddenly I realized that I had thrown myself at my boss, a man with whom I had only the most superficial of working relationships, a man I had on a pedestal. Ever since I'd gone into journalism and realized what editors did in putting together a newspaper every day, I had been in awe of them. And here I was, hanging all over my editor like a Southern belle with the vapors. I pulled back in embarrassment but was glad when he kept a comforting hand on my shoulder.

"Don, there's a body in my trunk," I said.

"I noticed. Who is he?"

I glared at him. "Why does everyone think I know him?"

"It *is* your car."

"That doesn't mean I know him! I suppose you think I put him there, too?"

"Did you?" asked the policeman.

I blinked, my anger gone as quickly as it had come.

"You don't really think I did, do you?" I could feel the handcuffs already.

The policeman shrugged. "Someone put him there."

"Well, it wasn't me." I hoped I sounded confident. "If he were really my body, I'd put him in someone else's car." I looked from the policeman to Don. "That only makes sense, right?"

The policeman shrugged.

Don smiled.

I shivered. "I think I'll go inside."

I sat forlornly in my living room for a few minutes

seeing the bright light from the generators through the tall windows. That was a nice thing about old buildings—tall windows.

Restless, I got up, went to my minuscule kitchen and put some water on to boil. People would be in soon, and hot drinks would be welcomed. Personally, I still wanted my Coke and Oreos, but there was no way I had the nerve to get a can from the trunk, even if they let me.

Ten minutes later, the policeman, whose name was Sergeant William Poole, sat carefully in my blue wing chair, his hair hanging damply on his forehead and his shirt gaping a bit about the belly. A mug full of coffee sat on the end table beside him, and he had a clipboard in one hand and a pen in the other. "All right, Miss Kramer, tell me all about it. In fact, why don't you tell me about your whole day."

I nodded. "Okay." I cleared my throat nervously. "This morning I drove my car to Taggart's garage for its annual state inspection. Jolene Meister, the secretary from work, picked me up at the garage at six forty-five."

"Where do you work?"

"At *The News*."

"Then he's your boss?" Sergeant Poole nodded at Don Eldredge, who was sitting comfortably on the sofa.

"Yes, he's my boss."

"You been at *The News* long?"

"About three months. I started just after Labor Day."

"What do you do?"

"I'm a general reporter and feature writer." Which sounded more glamorous than the gofer I often felt like.

"Have you lived in Amhearst long?"

"Since Labor Day weekend."

"Where do you come from?"

"The Pittsburgh area."

Sergeant Poole nodded. "Did you leave a family in Pittsburgh?"

"My parents and Sam, my younger brother, who's at Penn State." *And Jack,* I thought. *And Jack.*

"So you took your car to be inspected this morning. Why'd you go to Taggart's?"

"The people at work recommended that garage. No huge bill for unnecessary work, you know?" I noticed I was picking nervously at my cuticles and forced myself to stop. "Lots of garages like to bleed single women, but they told me Mr. Taggart wouldn't do that."

Sergeant Poole nodded like he knew Mr. Taggart and agreed. "When'd you get your car back, Miss Kramer?"

"Jolene dropped me off on her way home. I hadn't expected to be able to leave by five because of a late-afternoon meeting I was to cover and write up, but the meeting was canceled."

I gulped some tea, then continued. "Mr. Taggart wasn't around when Jolene dropped me off, but my car was waiting, the new inspection stickers on the window and the bill on the seat, just like we'd arranged when we thought I'd be late." I shrugged. "I just climbed in and drove off. After dinner at Ferretti's, I covered the Board of Education meeting at the high school. Then I came home."

"Did you have dinner with anyone?"

I shook my head. "I ate alone."

"You didn't stop for those sodas sometime between picking up your car and coming home?"

"No, I bought them yesterday. I just hadn't taken them out of the trunk."

Sergeant Poole nodded. "Did anything else significant happen today?"

I realized that, in place of my cuticles, I was playing with the string from my sweatshirt hood. I tucked it inside so I couldn't fiddle with it anymore and said, "I almost had an accident on my way home when some guy pulled out in front of me over on Oak Lane. But I didn't." I paused, thought, then shrugged my shoulders. "That's it."

Sergeant Poole chewed the tip of his pen for a minute, wrote something down, then asked, "Does the name Patrick Marten mean anything to you?"

"Patrick Marten?" I thought for a few minutes, then shook my head. "I don't know anyone by that name. Why? Is he the man in the trunk?"

Sergeant Poole nodded.

Patrick Marten. I sighed. Was there a Mrs. Patrick Marten somewhere waiting for him to come home? Were there kids? Certainly there was a mother and a father. A girlfriend? Obviously there was an enemy.

By the time Sergeant Poole capped his pen and hefted himself to his feet, I was feeling more normal. I almost smiled as the gaps in his shirt slid shut. After all, I was used to talking with people in living rooms. It was just corpses in the rain that bothered me.

And I had finally realized that I was in the middle of the biggest story of my fledgling journalism career.

"I'm sure we'll be talking again, Miss Kramer." Sergeant Poole pulled on his still-dripping slicker.

"Maybe tomorrow when you stop in to sign your statement."

"Whenever you want, Sergeant Poole."

He stopped and turned at the door. "By the way, we're going to have to impound your car for at least a few days."

I stared in consternation. "My car?" How could I investigate a murder without a car?

Don spoke for the first time. "I'll pick you up tomorrow morning, Merry, and take you to one of the local car dealers who leases as well as sells. We'll charge it to *The News*."

I nodded as I almost pushed Sergeant Poole out the door. What other unforeseen complications hunkered down just out of sight, eager to pounce?

But who cared about complications? I had a *story!*

"Don," I began.

"Yes?" His voice was full of suppressed emotion. If I didn't know better, I'd have thought he was laughing at me.

I glared at him. "You don't even know what I'm going to say."

"Of course I do," he said. "I sat on your sofa and watched you go from scared victim to professional reporter. You want to cover this story."

"You bet I do! It's the story of a lifetime, and I'm the perfect one for it! Who better?'

"Do you think you can handle it?"

"Can I handle it? Of course I can!" I was too excited to be mad at the suggestion that I couldn't.

Don grinned at me as he patted his carefully barbered graying hair. Everything about him was neat and precise, even the tidily folded scarf resting on the chair back. He shook it out and draped it about his neck, making sure the ends were even.

"To be honest, as soon as I heard the call on the police scanner at the office, I knew we had a winner. If you have any trouble as the story develops—" He held up his hand at my indignant look. "*If* you have any trouble, Mac can help you."

Don took his mug to the kitchen, and I heard him rinse it out. I stood in the middle of the living room and grinned like an idiot. I had a *story!*

I made myself act professionally as I walked Don to the door. I even made a pretty speech. "Thanks for being here when I talked to Sergeant Poole, Don. Something about a policeman always makes me feel guilty even when I'm innocent, which is all the time— except for the time I got a speeding ticket for going forty-five in a twenty-five mile zone."

Don laughed. "You've got nothing to worry about, Merry. I'll vouch for your character if they ever begin to suspect you."

"And my whereabouts," I said, suddenly remembering Don eating spaghetti at Ferretti's, talking intently with some unknown man. I hadn't approached him because the two of them looked so involved. In fact, I deliberately sat with my back to him. "That is, if you saw me like I saw you."

Don hesitated, then shook his head. "No, I don't think so."

I shrugged. "Oh, well, I doubt it matters. Thanks again for being here."

I watched him drive up the alley, then locked my

door carefully. I washed my mug and Sergeant Poole's and decided there was no way I was going to take the trash out. I didn't care that the police were still in the parking area. I was in for the night!

I checked and rechecked the doors and the windows, the tall, breakable windows that suddenly seemed less wonderful than usual. It was when I tested them for the fourth time that I noticed the moon peeking through the running clouds. The storm was over.

I got into bed with Whiskers and plumped the pillows carefully against the headboard. When I leaned back with my lined pad on my lap, Whiskers promptly climbed onto the pad.

"Not now, baby," I said, lifting the heavy creature and setting him down beside me. "I've got to write everything down before I forget it. Who knows?" I grinned at him. "Maybe I'll even write a true-crime book about this someday."

Whiskers yawned hugely, and I tickled him beneath the chin. I had selected him at the pound because he kept coming to me to be petted, purring whenever my hand even reached toward him. Now he lay close against me, a comforting presence after an unbeliev-able night.

I turned to my pad, feeling ghoulish as all my journalistic juices flowed and excitement coursed through me—now that I didn't have to look at the body again. Admittedly, what had happened was a great tragedy, especially for Patrick Marten. *But a great story is a great story and deserves to be written about,* I told myself hard-heartedly. In all great stories people suffer. If I could just get the information together, find the motive, the means, and the murderer, certainly I would reduce the suffering for Patrick Marten's family and friends. If Don was hugely impressed with my work, that was just a small extra.

Satisfied that I had manipulated my motives well, I wrote:

1. Took car to Mr. Taggart's. Spoke with him for a few minutes about its tendency to overheat.

2. Jolene picked me up. She never got out of her car. We were five minutes late for work.

3. Spent the morning opening mail and running dumb errands for Don and Mac. Felt trapped without my car.

4. Went to the mall in Exton with Mac to look for a camera over lunch. He made a pass. I rejected it. He asked me out. I said no. We laughed. I don't think he's mad even though he's famous for his grouchiness. Certainly he's not mad enough to put a body in my trunk. I bought the automatic-focus digital camera he recommended, which pleased him. I'm now broke.

5. Mac dropped me at Premier Medical, the new private emergency service, for an interview. Spent an hour with Drs. Mitchell and Wenger. Learned lots of new terms and used my new camera. The pix look good.

6. Called a taxi. Went back to the paper. Did telephone interviews with the head nurse at the hospital's trauma center and with three doctors in private practice. I really ought to find a doctor. What if I get sick?

7. Wrote up the story. Gave it to Don. He didn't moan too much.

8. Walked to Mayor Trudy McGilpin's office to observe a meeting between her, the water authority people and the recreational people. The meeting was canceled because Trudy's sick. I walked back to *The News*. Is Trudy as good as a lawyer as she appears to be as a mayor? How old is she? Forty?

9. Since I had no meeting to write up, I left much earlier than I'd planned. Jolene, the chatter queen, dropped me at Taggart's at about 5:20.

10. Got my car. I saw no one at all at the garage. I just took the car and left.

11. Stopped at Ferretti's Ristorante for some spaghetti. Delicious. Saw Don but he didn't see me. Did the Philadelphia *Inquirer* crossword puzzle while I ate. I couldn't decide whether I'm still lonely or not— which I guess is a good sign.

12. Went to the Board of Education meeting at the high school and arrived on time! High drama when the man in charge of the athletic committee started yelling at the woman in charge of the curriculum com-

mittee because she wanted too many books and accelerated classes. She will ruin the school and the budget that way, he said.

13. Left the high school about 10:25.
14. A wild ride home. Almost hit a man on Oak when some guy pulled out in front of me. What if I'd had an accident with that body in the trunk?
15. Got to my apartment about 10:45.
16. Found Patrick Marten at 10:47.
17. Got the shakes at 10:49.
18. Cops arrived at 11:05.
19. Questions:

   • Was the body in the trunk when I got the car at the garage? It must have been.

   • Who put it there? Mr. Taggart? A nice old man like him?

   • Why did someone put it in *my* car? Because he/she doesn't like me? No one around Amhearst knows me well enough yet to dislike me. And no one's ever disliked me like that my whole life.

   • Or maybe he/she doesn't like *The News?* But who would know that my car was the car of a *News* reporter? There's nothing written on the doors or anything.

   • Maybe it just happened because the car was handy? That means it was someone at Taggart's, doesn't it? Or was it someone driving by who happened to need a place to get rid of a body? It was dark even before I got there. Winter solstice

approaching and all that. He could have
just dumped Patrick and run. But how did
he get the trunk open? My extra set of
keys was locked in the car. Did the
murderer lock the keys in the car after he
left Patrick, and I just assumed Mr.
Taggart put them there?

A huge yawn interrupted my note taking. I didn't
bother to smother it even when Whiskers looked at
me askance.

I glanced at my clock—1:45 a.m. I groaned.
Morning would be here all too soon. I turned out my
light and lay down. Whiskers came to sleep in the depression between my shoulder and the pillow.

I closed my eyes and saw a man in a green jacket
lying on cases of soda. Instantly I was wide-awake,
afraid to close my eyes again. I stared unhappily at the
ceiling and jumped every time Whiskers moved.

"Stay still, baby," I said, scratching his ears. He
purred happily and began grooming himself. The bed
shook with each slurp.

I put my hand between his tongue and body. "Not
now, Whiskers."

He purred again and began licking my hand. I
pulled away from the rasping wetness, and the cat
continued on his paw without missing a beat.

I sighed. The sensible thing would be to kick the
animal out of bed, but much to my surprise I felt a
strong need for his warm presence.

I reached out and turned on my light. In the brightness, my shoulders relaxed, and the world righted itself.

I looked around carefully, finding exactly what I knew was there: nothing. I lay back and flicked off the light again. I turned it back on immediately.

"Don't tell anyone," I told Whiskers as he blinked at the brightness, "but we're sleeping with the light on."

THREE

Last night's storm had indeed blown itself out to sea, leaving behind a thin coating of ice that caused a one-hour delay in school openings and a massive slow-down for morning commuters.

True to his word, Don picked me up and took me to arrange for a rental car. He solidified his place in my heart when he said, "Charge it to *The News*."

"I need your piece on the murder by nine," Don said as we left the car dealer. "Make it personal, real human interest. Mac will write a parallel news piece. You'll both be front page."

I nodded. *The News* was a twelve- to sixteen-page afternoon paper, which meant we scheduled news deadlines at nine, editing deadlines at ten, and it was printed and ready for delivery by noon. Don took personally any news that broke between ten and three because it couldn't make the paper, yet readers expected to see it there.

"The Board of Education stuff?" I asked.

"Anything scandalous?"

"Just fighting over where to spend the money."

He nodded. "So what else is new? Write it up for

tomorrow. And don't miss that interview with that artist."

I groaned inwardly. A personality puff piece was the last thing I wanted to do now.

"Hey, his upcoming exhibit is going to be a big civic occasion." Don apparently detected my mood. "Mayor McGilpin would be very unhappy if we overlooked it. Got to show Amhearst in a good light, you know."

I nodded, grinning. "Especially after a murder."

Don grunted. "And give me another human-interest piece for Friday about the murder. Interview the family. Find a wife or parents or brothers or sisters. Find out what a wonderful guy he was or what a louse he was. Is he local? If so, find teachers and old friends. If not, find out how he came to be here in Amhearst."

I nodded again. Three angles or points of view, an old reporter had told me when I first started working back in Pittsburgh. For any human-interest story or information piece, find three perspectives on the story to give it enough depth. Parents, teachers, friends? Wife, employer, brother? His past, present and lack of future?

Of course, those interviews would have an emotional cost, both for those who had cared about Patrick Marten and for me, but I put that thought out of my mind as soon as it appeared.

I drove my rental to the office, thankful for a heater that worked quickly, because the sun, though shining brightly, had little warmth. I scanned the clear blue sky when the radio weatherman announced that another storm was due tomorrow. Chicago was already snowed under, he reported in the cheery voice of a committed skier, and the formidable flow of frigid Canadian air showed no signs of weakening before it reached the East Coast. I could practically hear him rubbing his hands together in anticipation of driving to the Poconos over treacherous roads for the thrill of throwing himself down mountains on strips of wood or whatever composites skis were made of these days.

I should live in Florida or Arizona so I need never be cold again. Even if I stayed in Pennsylvania, I had promised myself I would be intelligent about it and never, ever, ski.

Finally I settled down at my desk. *Murder,* I typed, *is a distant crime that involves other people. Last night, to my utter surprise and distress, it involved me.*

I looked at my CRT and reread my opening. Don was a stickler for a hard lead on news pieces, the traditional, journalistic inverted pyramid of who, what, where, when and why. But he seemed at ease with soft leads on special pieces like mine was to be. One thing was certain: he'd tell me if he was unhappy.

I had my copy on his desk before nine, and then I gave my mom a quick call. It was only a matter of time before she and Dad heard about last night, and I thought they should hear the story from me.

"Merry! Oh, Merry!" Mom was predictably distressed.

"I'm fine, Mom. I'm absolutely fine. And safe. Believe me."

There was a small silence, and I could hear her skepticism zip clearly across the miles from Pittsburgh to Amhearst.

"Well, I've got to go," I said quickly. "I've got an important interview." And I hung up.

Sighing, I forced myself to begin planning my interview with artist Curtis Carlyle. I could hardly resist smiling every time I said his name. It was too perfect to belong to anyone other than an artist or a movie star or some other arty, public person. Had his mother been prescient, or did she just like alliteration? Was he named after a rich uncle, or had he made up the name to create a persona?

As I jotted my notes, I thought how incredible it was that I should do something as bizarre as find a body one night and something as routine as interview some local artist the next morning. Variety like this was one of the reasons I loved newspaper work.

Curtis Carlyle. Artist. Watercolors. One-man art show scheduled for Friday night and Saturday in the Brennan Room at City Hall in Amhearst. Chester County scenes his specialties, notably winter scenes with old stone barns and houses, wonderful skies. Former gym teacher. Still coached high school soccer and tennis.

Usually interviews intrigued me, and I looked forward to them. Finding out what made people tick was like opening locked doors. Always a new room appeared, and sometimes unexpected treasure. Today's was an exception. How could an artist—even one with a name like his—compare with a murder? I found myself wishing I could skip him and get back to my murder investigation.

The last of the ice was melted by ten in the morning when I pulled up in front of Curtis Carlyle's house, odd puddles the only reminders of the bad weather.

I studied the brick-faced ranch, looking for clues about its occupant. It looked much like the other houses in the neighborhood, not the retreat of an artist of some stature.

Thin sunlight patterned the roof through the barren branches of the beech and poplar that formed a semicircle around the lawn. Brown, frosty, winter-killed grass tufted the deep front yard. On the half acres to the right and left were other ranches very similar in appearance. Across the street a pair of three-year-olds made fat and unbendable by their snowsuits stared at me from the porch of yet another ranch.

I looked again at Carlyle's house and shrugged. It told me nothing.

I rang the bell and waited. No response. I rang again as I checked my watch. Ten o'clock. That was the time we had agreed on. Could he have forgotten? Sure, he was probably busy with last-minute arrangements for his show, but I was as important to him as he was to me. If I could tear myself away from a murder investigation to make time for him, certainly he could return the compliment. After all, he needed the exposure as much as I needed the article.

I rang a third time. Maybe he was hard of hearing. It seemed to me that anyone who retired from teaching must have lost something through the years of dealing with kids. I would have thought it would be sanity, but hearing was a distinct possibility.

Suddenly the door imploded and a huge bear of a man filled the opening. A great smile lit his face, crinkling his eyes to slits behind their dark-framed glasses.

"Merrileigh Kramer from *The News,* right?" he

asked as he threw the storm door open for me. "Hi. I'm Curt Carlyle."

I nodded as I stepped by him, quickly revising my erroneous preconceptions. "Former gym teacher" obviously didn't mean what I had thought. Curt Carlyle was no retiree; he was a man in his early thirties who exuded energy, whose mass of curly dark hair was a far cry from the sparse gray I had anticipated.

"Do you mind if we talk downstairs?" he asked. "I'm finishing up some things for tomorrow."

He led the way downstairs and as we descended, he began to whistle "Row, Row, Row Your Boat." I grimaced.

Unexpectedly, a huge, bright room greeted me. The rear wall of the walkout basement was exposed by the downward slope of the lawn and had been lined with glass. The lemon light of winter was aided by great lights hanging over Carlyle's worktable. Shelves lining the front wall of the room were filled with art supplies from paper and paints to huge rolls of popcorn plastic used for packaging. It was a roll of the wrap that he was working with now, swathing a framed picture four feet by three for safe transport.

I pulled out my new camera and began snapping him as he worked. He was happy to pose at his worktable and stood easily beside a wonderfully detailed watercolor of a stone barn backed by a brooding, stormy sky, dark clouds streaked dramatically with the brilliant oranges and yellows of an angry setting sun.

"This is the original of the picture I'm offering prints of this year." He wiped an imaginary speck off the glass before he began wrapping it in plastic. "I select one picture a year to reproduce, and I've been pleasantly surprised at how successful the prints have been."

"How many prints do you make?"

"Five hundred. Each numbered and signed."

"I know you're a former gym teacher," I said. "How did you end up being a watercolorist?"

"I've always loved painting, but it didn't seem like a very practical way to make a living. So I went with my other love, sports, and taught. In my late twenties I became very dissatisfied. I had visions of me rolling out the ball for the rest of my life while others played."

I imagined him stalking the sidelines like a tethered grizzly, frustrated and unhappy.

"My sister, Joan, was the one who encouraged me to take the leap." He nodded toward the portrait of an attractive woman I had assumed to be a wife or girl-friend. "So what if I had a couple of lean years, she said. I had only myself to feed. Our parents had left us this house, and since Joan was married, she urged me to live here and go for it." He shrugged and grinned happily. "I did, and though I've been hungry a few times, I don't regret it. Life's exciting again."

"Your sister must be very proud," I said.

His smile disappeared. "I'm sure she would be, but she died two years ago, just before things really started to move for me."

"Oh. I'm sorry," I said.

"Don't feel bad, Merrileigh. It's okay. She was a strong Christian, and that thought comforts me." He smiled and began to whistle again.

I listened to him for a minute, then said sharply, "Do you know what you're doing?"

He looked at me in surprise.

"You're whistling," I said.

"I beg your pardon?"

"Everyone does it, and it drives me crazy." I tried not to grind my teeth. "Though most people usually sing."

"What in the world are you talking about?" Curt asked.

"What were you whistling?" I demanded.

He thought a moment. "'Merrily We Roll Along.'"

"Right. And what were you whistling when we came down the steps?"

"I don't know," he said patiently. "What?"

"'Row, Row, Row Your Boat'!"

Curt looked at me as though I were unstable.

"It drives me wild," I said. "Sometimes I'd like to strangle my mother."

Suddenly Curt's face cleared and he began to laugh. "Merrily/Merrileigh, right?"

I nodded. "Most people do it subconsciously, though some people actually do it on purpose just to bother me."

Jack had been one of those people, and I'd never understood why he intentionally did something I disliked so much.

"It doesn't matter whether you think I'm overreacting or not, Jack," I said to him once. "Just please believe me when I say I hate it!"

And he'd smiled his knee-weakening smile and sung back to me to the tune of "Row, Row, Row Your Boat":

"Calm, calm, calm yourself. Don't get so upset. Merrileigh, Merrileigh, Merrileigh, I don't like to see you fret."

I looked stormily at Curt Carlyle, who smiled unrepentantly back.

"I'll try to resist," he said. "If I do slip, tell me, and I'll shape up right away. Do people call you something besides Merrileigh to help then deny the word association?"

I was suddenly embarrassed about my outburst and how childish I sounded. It must have been last night's shock.

"People usually call me Merry," I said, and sighed. "I'm sorry, but if you'd lived with those songs every day of your life since the teacher first called your name aloud in kindergarten, you'd have developed a complex, too."

"I'm sure I would have," Curt agreed amiably.

He seemed to be studying me. My hand went to my spikey hair, but it stuck out above my head as it should. I glanced down at my gray slacks, jade sweater and navy blazer. They weren't covered with Whiskers's hair, so they looked all right to me. I sucked discreetly at the gap between my teeth. I hadn't eaten anything since I'd brushed, but I always worried since the spinach-in-the-teeth fiasco eight years ago. I cleared my throat self-consciously.

"Don't I know you from somewhere?" Curt asked.

I lifted an eyebrow and looked at him in surprise. "Isn't that line a bit old?"

"I'm not giving you a line," Curt said earnestly. "I honestly think I know you from somewhere."

"Oh. Well. I don't think so," I said. "I've only lived in Amhearst since the beginning of September."

He shook his head and squinted at me.

I flipped my notebook open and asked, "Don't you find painting and coaching a strange combination?"

He took the hint and got right to the issue at hand.

"Painting and coaching are good foils for each other if you think about it. Painting is creative and energizing and sedentary and solitary. Coaching is restorative and repetitious and active and social."

By the time the interview drew to a close thirty minutes later, I knew Curt laughed a lot, talked with his hands and had a lot of work still to do for tomorrow night's opening.

"This article will be in Friday's paper," he told me, as if it was his choice. "Right?"

"Probably Saturday's edition," I said.

"I'd like it to be in tomorrow's."

"I don't think you get to choose. It's the editor's call." I smiled so I wouldn't sound defensive, but I hate it when people try to tell me what to do with the articles about them, especially since I have no control over when anything is printed, only when it's written. "If it comes out Saturday, I can cover the opening tomorrow night and people can read about it in time to stop in Saturday if they wish."

He nodded, not overly happy but wisely recognizing that he had no say in the issue. "Why don't you come and see the chaos tonight or tomorrow morning? Then by contrast, the professionalism of tomorrow night will really impress you— I hope."

"Thanks," I said. "I'll have to see. I know I can't

come tonight, but maybe tomorrow. It depends on what else I'm assigned to do."

"Tell Don I said to let you come," said Curt.

"You know Don?" I asked.

Curt's smile dimmed. "Yes. I know Don."

FOUR

I returned to *The News* to find the office in an uproar. Don was waving his hands as he talked to Mac Carnuccio. Mac was listening intently, looking like the proverbial thundercloud. Larry Schimmer, the sports guy, and Edie Whatley, the family and entertainment editor, were deep in conversation at Edie's desk. Edie was wiping at tears that continued to flow despite her mopping efforts.

I stopped at Jolene's desk. She was staring at her computer screen, the earplug for her transcriber in place, but she wasn't working.

"What's wrong?" I asked.

Jolene transferred her blank stare to me. She had gorgeous skin, great brown eyes that she dramatized expertly, and enough hair to make Dolly Parton jealous, though Jolene's was a rich chestnut. "Oh, Merry, isn't it terrible?"

"What? What's wrong?"

"It's Trudy McGilpin. She's dead."

"Trudy? Trudy the *mayor?* But all she had was the flu! At least that's what they told us yesterday evening at her office when she didn't show up for the meeting."

Jolene nodded. "But she died sometime last night. We got a call about it just a few minutes ago. She didn't keep her morning appointments, and her secretary couldn't reach her by phone. She got worried and went to Trudy's, and—" Jolene paused, then continued with great drama. "And there she was."

I sympathized with the unknown secretary. I knew that finding bodies could take the starch out of the crispest individual.

Jolene, whose husband had just left her, took a long and shaky breath. "That just shows what happens when you live alone."

I blinked. "I doubt that living alone did her in, but she must have been a lot sicker than anyone realized."

"A lot," agreed Jolene as she coughed delicately and leaned toward me. "I don't feel like I have a fever, do I?"

I looked at her carefully made-up face and her clear eyes.

"You look fine to me, Jolene."

She leaned forward some more, one hand raising her bangs off her forehead. "I don't know. Check for me."

I placed a couple of fingers on her cool forehead and looked thoughtful.

"I knew it," she said, distressed. "I'm getting sick."

"You're fine," I said.

"But you frowned."

"I was thinking about Trudy," I said.

"Well, think about me. Do I have a fever?"

I shook my head. "You do not."

She didn't believe me. "But I know I'm getting sick."

"Merry!" Don's voice boomed across the room. "Come here. And, Mac, I need you, too."

Thank you, Don! I eagerly left the sick bay.

The News office space was cramped, old and reeked of smoke in spite of the fact that no one had been allowed to smoke in the room for at least five years. The desks were battered and scarred, the linoleum pattern had worn off decades ago and the file cabinets were dented and scratched. Only the lighting and the computer system were modern, and they were both state-of-the-art.

The other highly unique aspect of the newsroom was the greenery. Plants sat on every available surface and on some they shouldn't. And every plant was lush and full and in better health than I was. I could only imagine what Don paid a service to tend these beauties, though why he wanted them in the first place, I didn't know.

I dodged Larry's and Edie's desks, the fiche machine and the soda and coffee machines. The latter two were placed near Don so he could keep an eye on loiterers. A Wandering Jew draped over the soda machine in such rampant health that I always thought of *Little Shop of Horrors* and the plant that ate people. I gave the machine and its decoration wide berth.

"You heard?" Don asked as I approached.

"About Trudy?" I nodded. "Jolene just told me."

I stared in surprise at my boss's large, cluttered desk. Cluttered? Don? Usually he sat in organized splendor in front of the huge window that looked down from the second-floor editorial offices onto the business district of Amhearst. If it weren't for the incontrovertible proof of the daily issues of *The News*, I'd think Don never worked, because his desk never showed it. Except now.

"I want you to do the personality obit. Contact family, friends, get some good quotes. You know. Mac will do the political and public-service analysis and contact the police and hospital."

"The police?" I said, startled.

"They're involved because it's an unwitnessed death. Mere form," said Mac. "I have to talk to them about your body, anyway."

"It's not my body!"

Mac grinned. "That's not what I heard."

"Mac, come on!"

"From what I hear, he seems about the right age for you." He gave his trademark leer.

I wasn't sure whether I should be offended by a joke about a dead man. "How old was he? And how old do you think I am?"

"I don't know about you, but he was twenty-five." Mac glanced at the notebook he had in his hand. "He lived at 594 Lyme Street with his mother, Liz, and worked as a grease jockey at Taggart's."

"So I got him at Taggart's garage?"

"I don't think the cops are certain yet, but that seems to be the theory they're working with."

"Excuse me, you two," said Don curtly, "but I think we were talking about Trudy."

I nodded, staring at my boss with interest. His hair was actually mussed where he had run a hand through it, revealing his incipient bald spot rather cruelly. I knew that if he could see himself, he'd be upset.

Don shuffled some papers into a haphazard pile. "Your articles about Trudy will be the leads in tomorrow's edition. I want them by nine a.m." He made a frustrated sound. "I hate it when a story breaks too late for the day's edition."

"Had Trudy known your feelings," said Mac harshly, "I'm certain she would have arranged things differently."

Don looked startled, like a mastiff bitten by a toy poodle. "You know I didn't mean it that way, Mac. You know I respected Trudy. Now get to work, both of you."

Mac and I turned away together, Mac still scowling. We walked across the office together, or as together as you can walk when there's only enough room for one person at a time between the furniture. When we reached his desk, he grabbed his coat from the back of his chair.

"Any chance of dinner to talk over this case?" he asked as he stuffed his arms in the sleeves.

"Which case?" I asked.

"Either one's okay with me," he said, jettisoning the scowl and smiling with great charm. "It's the company I'm interested in."

I didn't doubt that for an instant, and I was equally sure he wouldn't want to stop with dinner. "I'm sorry," I said. "I'm busy tonight."

He looked at me skeptically, but I just smiled sweetly. I wasn't about to tell him that my business was a rehearsal at church. I knew what he'd think of that.

Mac's eyes slid over my shoulder and hardened as he looked at Don.

"He's one cold fish," Mac said. "A real iceberg."

I turned and looked again at Don's mussed hair and cluttered desk. I didn't know about *iceberg*. I thought he was distressed and trying not to show it. It just leaked out in spite of himself. When I turned to say so, Mac was already rushing out the back door, scarf streaming over his shoulder.

I shrugged and went to my desk, thinking about the disadvantages of being new in town. Who should I call about Trudy? What if I called someone and he hadn't heard yet, and I had to break the news to him? I shivered at that terrible thought.

To put such a possibility off as long as possible, I clicked my way into *The News*'s e-library and typed Trudy's name. I wasn't surprised at the wealth of information I found, but most was more what Mac would use than what I needed. Still, here and there I found items that spoke of her as a woman, not a politician or a lawyer.

Next I skimmed the paper's electronic archives, but they only went back to 1988. I moved to FotoWeb and looked at photos of a vibrant and lovely woman. I was stopped cold by a particularly riveting shot of Trudy in an evening gown, dancing at the annual hospital gala, laughing at something her partner had said.

I rose abruptly and went to the file drawers against the far wall. I pushed the huge jade plant sitting on top back against the wall and opened the *M* drawer, pulling out the McGilpin file. In these old clips, I should find names as well as some good background information for my piece. I returned to my desk and began reading. The clipping service had done a good job; there was plenty of material available.

Trudy was a local girl, raised in Amhearst, a graduate of Amhearst High School where she was president of her senior class and star of the spring musical. In the pictures of the musical, she looked fresh and pretty, her young face eager and alive. "A glowing talent," the review of the play read. "Amhearst's own Julie Andrews."

Since the writer of the review was a woman named Alice McGilpin, I suspected a strong case of family prejudice.

Trudy attended the University of Pennsylvania as an undergraduate, no mean feat for a small-town girl who was to be her family's first college graduate. She received her law degree with honors from Dickinson Law School. When she returned to Amhearst, she joined the local law firm of Grassley and Jordan, now Grassley, Jordan and McGilpin, where she developed a specialty in divorce and family issues.

Perhaps, I thought, *dealing with all the tensions and hatreds between people who had promised to love each other forever had been enough to keep her from marrying.*

Picture after picture showed how active in community affairs Trudy had been, sitting on the boards of the YWCA and the hospital and chairing the local United Way drive. She was in the final year of her first three-year term as mayor and had been planning to run again. A popular mayor, she undoubtedly would have won easily.

There were a brother and sister-in-law who lived in Goshen, about fifteen miles east, and parents retired in Florida.

I knew there was no way I would be hard-boiled enough to contact the parents (what if they hadn't heard yet?), but I could call the brother, Stanton McGilpin. Also I would contact either Mr. Grassley or

Mr. Jordan at their law office, one or two of the city commissioners who served with Trudy—one in her party, one in the opposition—the director of the Y, and the chairman of the hospital board. At least that last one would be easy; the chairman was Don Eldredge.

I approached his desk and wondered again how he felt about the double tier of African violets that lined the sill of the great window by which he sat. Did he have purple, rose, lavender, pink, white and variegated dreams and wonder why? Somehow the violets were so un-Don, yet they flourished beside him.

"I need a quote from you about Trudy," I said.

Don looked up, surprised, and I noted that his hair was once again perfect. "From me?" he said. "What for?"

"She served on the hospital board, and you're the chairman."

"Oh," he said. "Okay. Just say something about what a good and capable worker she was, and how she dedicated great amounts of time to the hospital and its needs. She will be sorely missed by all of us."

I walked back to my desk, jotting Don's comments as I walked. Pretty trite for a professional journalist.

Next I called Grassley, Jordan and McGilpin. The secretary who answered was obviously trying not to cry into the phone. She kept sniffing and hiccuping. When she realized who I was, she began talking about Trudy.

"She was the best boss in the world, she was. So pleasant. Always please and thank you. And attractive. Real class, you know? I could never figure out why she wasn't married." Obviously being married was important to the secretary. "But I think she had a new boyfriend. She was smiling a lot more." And the girl began to cry in earnest.

The line went empty, and I thought I had been disconnected. Almost immediately, though, a male voice boomed over the phone, speaking too enthusiastically as a cover for his emotions.

"Trudy was wonderful," he said. "A fine lawyer, interested in her clients and very knowledgeable in law. She was a strong woman, but not at the expense of her femininity. She more than held her own in a courtroom. We shall miss her very much."

"Thank you," I said. "And to whom am I speaking?"

"This is Edmund Grassley." His voice broke on the last syllable of his name, and he cleared his throat. "We're going to miss her very much," he whispered, and hung up.

My eyes misted at the man's genuine emotion, and I couldn't help glancing at too-cool Don, sitting at his desk in reorganized splendor.

Nick Dominic and Forbes Raleigh, the commissioners, and Annie Parmalee, the director of the YWCA, said much the same thing as Don and Mr. Grassley, surprise, surprise. They were all greatly saddened by Trudy's death and would miss her. Amhearst was diminished by her passing. How hard it was to put deep emotion into quotes.

Finally, when I could avoid it no longer, I called Stanton McGilpin.

"I'm sorry. He's not here right now," said a woman. "May I take a message?"

"I'm Merrileigh Kramer from *The News*. I'm calling in reference to the death of Mr. McGilpin's sister. We will be devoting much of tomorrow's paper to Trudy, and we thought he might like to make a statement, sort of a eulogy."

There was a small silence. Then, "I'll tell him you called."

I started to say thank you, but the line was dead. I doubted I'd ever hear from Stanton McGilpin, and I couldn't blame him.

Still, contacting a family member in one context made me think about doing the same thing in another. I grabbed the phone book, looked up a number and dialed before my nerve failed.

"Mrs. Marten, my name is Merrileigh Kramer. I was wondering if I might speak to you about your son's death."

A weary voice asked, "Are you from the police?"

"No. I work at *The News*."

"They're going to keep putting him in the paper whether I talk to you or not, aren't they?"

"A crime like this will certainly be covered." I kept my voice neutral. I couldn't tell whether Mrs. Marten was happy or distressed that Patrick was to get so much posthumous media attention.

Her sigh echoed down the phone line. "Come over if you want. I'd like to be certain that Patrick is pre-sented as the fine kid he was. But don't come until tomorrow. I can't talk to anyone else today. I'm too busy crying."

FIVE

Labor Day Sunday had been my first Sunday in Amhearst. It had been a hot, sunny, end-of-summer day, and I attended Faith Community Church. While I waited in the hot sanctuary for the service to begin, I read a notice in the bulletin that a bell choir was being formed.

"If you are interested, a free ring clinic will be held Friday night at seven-thirty to provide a chance to try ringing and to provide information about the bell choir," the notice read.

Friday night came, and I ate alone at McDonald's: a cheeseburger, small fries, large Diet Coke and package of cookies. Very healthful. Then I went home to the first night of my first full weekend in my new apartment and held a one-sided conversation with Whiskers.

"So how was your day, baby? Did you get enough rest? I must apologize for not saving you any of my French fries. Before I realized what was happening, I'd eaten them all. Every last bite. Forgive me?"

He rolled over on the bed and offered his tummy for a rub, a sure sign that he wasn't upset. Not that

Whiskers was ever impolite, even when I disappointed him. He was the very soul of civility, listening whenever I talked, just like he understood. I chose to believe that he was interested in my thoughts, rather than accept the more obvious conclusion that he was hoping I'd offer him more food if he listened long enough.

That September night I was still full of doubts about my move and not at all certain that striking out on my own had been such a good idea after all. For years, Friday nights meant Jack and a night out and laughter and—on more than one occasion—tears. But always something.

Now there was nothing. I sighed as I puttered around, straightening up where there was no mess. My little apartment had a living room across the front, a dining room and a small kitchen, a bedroom and a unique bathroom. The bathroom had doors that opened into both the bedroom behind it and the living room in front of it. Neither door had a lock. I hadn't quite figured out how you avoided being ambushed from one side or the other when there was company, but more than likely that wasn't a problem I'd have to deal with for quite some time.

"Oh, Whiskers!" I despaired as I flopped into a chair. "I'm so lonely!" He climbed up and settled in my lap, purring contentedly.

Of course you're contented, I thought as I stroked him. *It was me or the pound, and anyone'd pick me. Wouldn't they? Wouldn't he? Wouldn't Jack? Why wouldn't Jack?*

I stood abruptly, dumping Whiskers. That waylaid

self-pity and failure. I was now strong. Independent. My own woman.

Dear God, I prayed, *don't let me fail because of loneliness and boredom and self-pity. I want to press on!*

And I suddenly understood that pressing on had a price. Staying in Pittsburgh would have cost me dearly, too, but at least I knew that price—life passing me by, emotional stunting, Jack as God.

One night two years before, my father had come to my room. He stood in the doorway looking concerned.

"Merry, you know Jack better than we do, so tell me how things stand between you two. You've been dating pretty much exclusively since your junior year at Penn State. Are you two serious? Or is he, as I fear and as I've said before, using up your young years with no thought of commitment?"

I laughed. "Dad, you needn't worry. Jack loves me, and I certainly love him. Things are moving well."

Dad looked unconvinced, but he said, "You know we only want you to be happy, honey."

"I know, Dad. I am."

But I lied, and Dad probably knew it. The trouble was that I didn't. I lived so stoically for so long with Jack's unwillingness to commit that I no longer recognized my own pain.

"I love you, Merry," Jack would say, "but I'm not ready to get married yet. Let's pray about it, and we'll decide in six months, okay? Let's just enjoy today."

And his melting smile and beguiling manner and earnest eyes would win my assent.

I might have continued to act the wimp forever if

my younger brother, Sam, hadn't forced me to see things differently and shamed me into taking my life back into my own hands. When he was a kid, Sam loved Jack, but in his later high school years Sam matured greatly. In fact, in many ways, he matured beyond Jack, who by this time was a handsome, charming man fast approaching thirty.

"He's always late, Merry, hours late sometimes, and he never calls to tell you," Sam said. "And he never apologizes. That's inconsiderate. I'd never do that to a girl I was dating."

"Don't let it bother you," I said. "It's just Jack's way. He has trouble with time."

"And you think that excuses his lack of respect?"

"It's okay." I patted his arm. "Really."

Or: "Does he ever ask you what you want to do, Merry? It seems to me you've watched an awful lot of church league basketball and baseball games, but I don't remember him taking you to a concert or anything you like. And he's always trailing his fan club of guys who are as irresponsible as he is. Who does he think you are? One of the boys?"

"Believe me, he knows I'm not one of the boys," I said. "And I like church league ball games. I can always listen to music on a CD or my iPod, but you can't see these games unless you're there."

"I'm not saying you shouldn't go to the games," Sam said. "I'm saying he should go to the concerts, too. For you."

"If I'm not bothered, Sam, then I don't think you need to be, either."

Or: "He's coming to get you in five minutes, and

he just called? Isn't he ever considerate enough to plan ahead? And aren't you smart enough to be unavailable? For heaven's sake, Merry, you were going shopping with Ellen and Joyce. Now you're going to let them down just to be here for him? How's he supposed to learn to appreciate you? You let him walk all over you! You're a marshmallow!"

"The girls understand that Jack comes first, Sam."

"He might come first with you. I just wonder if you really come first with him."

"Sam! How unkind!"

When Sam first started talking against Jack, I just ignored him. After all, what did he know about love? He was only a high school kid.

When I began to suspect that he might be right, I worked hard to plug my ears. I couldn't listen; that would be disloyal to Jack.

One memorable night this past July, Jack was scheduled to pick me up for my birthday dinner. We were going to Anna Maria's, where they served the best pasta in the world, and I was dressed in Jack's favorite dress.

"It makes your dark eyes flash and your skin glow," he'd told me once.

The last think I did as I got ready was tuck into my purse a letter I received that day about an article I'd done on children with AIDS.

"Perhaps people will understand my grief better because of your article," the mother of a stricken child had written. "I cannot thank you enough for your tenderness and accuracy."

I smiled with satisfaction. Even Jack would have to see that I'd done well.

Mom and Dad and Sam left about six-thirty for an evening with friends, and I waited patiently for Jack. At eight he hadn't arrived, nor had he called. Nine and no Jack. Ten. At ten-thirty, as I was rereading my fan letter for the umpteenth time to buck up my flagging spirits, the phone rang.

"Merry, I'm hungry."

"Me, too."

It was too late for Anna Maria's and fettucine Alfredo, but we could still get a Big Mac if we hurried. "Happy birthday" can sound sweet over special sauce, too.

"Come on over to my place and make us some eggs, okay?" Jack said.

So much for special sauce. I looked at my letter, folded it carefully and put it under the phone where it would be safe until I got home.

"Sure, Jack," I said softly. "Be right there."

What an idiot.

I opened the front door just as Mom and Dad and Sam crossed the porch.

"How was dinner?" Mom asked.

I hesitated. I knew how they would react to the news that Jack not only hadn't come for me, he had also asked me to come to him.

Asked? a little voice inside said. *Asked? How about told.*

It's nice to realize that some semblance of sanity remained, but at the time, I tried to squash it.

Sam, now a handsome eighteen-year-old three weeks short of leaving for Penn State, looked at me.

"You never went out," he said. "Right?"

The kid was too smart. Willing my chin not to tremble, I nodded.

"But you're going out now?" Mom asked. She looked around for Jack.

"He's not here, is he, Merry?" said Sam. "Jerky Jack isn't here. He never was here. What did he do? Forget?"

"No!" said I. "He called."

"Sure," said Sam sarcastically. "About five minutes ago, I bet. What was his excuse?"

"He didn't make any excuses," I said in a shaky voice.

"But if Jack's not here, where are you going?" Mom asked.

"To Jack's."

They all stared at me.

"He's hungry," I said, just as if that explained everything.

"Of course he is," Sam said. "Jerky Jack wants to eat Marshmallow Merry."

Dad reached out and laid a hand on Sam's arm. "Easy, son."

"Dad!" Sam was almost in tears. "He's making a fool of her!"

My father looked at me with pain in his eyes. I looked at the floor.

"Merry," Dad said, "do you know that you rarely laugh anymore?"

I looked up, startled. That wasn't what I expected him to say. I expected the heart-wrenching talk about Jack wasting my youth. I knew how to ignore that one.

"Do you realize that you have lost the gutsy independence that used to worry your mother and me so when you were in high school?"

"If I'm such a wimp," I said defensively, "how come I'm such a good journalist? Huh? That takes guts!"

He just smiled sadly. "Do you know that you put Jack ahead of everything, including common sense and God?"

I stared at the porch floor again. Deep inside I knew my father was right. I knew Sam was right. Somehow, I *had* become a spineless marshmallow. And not even a soft, spongy one that bounced back after it was squeezed, but a permanently mashed one whose heart ached all the time, especially when Jack told me that he loved me, but…

Mom put an arm around my waist and gently led me back into the house.

"You can't run to him whenever he calls, Merry," she said. "You know that. And he's not going to change, I'm afraid. He will always see life only from his own narrow point of view and act to satisfy only himself. It's a tragedy, because he's squandering a great potential for serving God by serving Jack, but that's how it is. Jack first and foremost."

I shivered in the July heat. I wrapped my arms around myself, trying vainly to get warm, as my mother continued relentlessly.

"You must face the fact, honey, that Jack's way of thinking leaves out a wife—which is probably a good thing, because she'd spend her life being hurt and Jack would never understand why."

"But I love him," I whispered. Tears filled my eyes. "I know things can't continue as they are, but I don't know what to do."

"Move," said Sam so quickly that he'd obviously been waiting for the chance to state his idea. "Go someplace where Jack isn't. If he cares enough, he'll come and get you. If he doesn't…" He shrugged.

I didn't go to Jack's that night. I also didn't sleep that night or for several more as I thought and prayed. Move! The very thought made me sweat. As a compromise, I got my hair cut.

"What have you done?" Jack asked angrily when he saw the shorn me.

"I got my hair cut," I said as he stalked around me. "Don't you like it?"

He shrugged. "It's okay, I guess, if you like girls with boys' haircuts."

I looked in the mirror at the young woman with curly, spiky black hair. "I do not look like a boy." I didn't look like me, either, but I figured I'd get to know this stranger in time.

He ignored me and got to what, for him, was the point. "You never asked me."

For some reason, for the first time in years, I got angry at Jack. "I'm twenty-six, Jack. I'm allowed to cut my hair with or without your consent."

The next day I went to the library when a story I was covering took me nearby. I read the want ads in the Philadelphia area papers. A week later I had a job at *The News* in Amhearst, thirty miles west of Philadelphia in Chester County. In two more weeks I was ready to move.

"But we never talked this over," Jack protested. "What if I don't want you to move? After all, we're thinking of getting married."

"We are? When?"

"Sure we are. I just need a few more months, that's all."

I shook my head. "I *have* to find out who I am, Jack, who God made me to be, because I've forgotten."

I determined when I first arrived in Amhearst that on work nights I would turn the TV off at ten and be in bed by ten-thirty. Discipline was absolutely necessary if I were to survive. The problem always came between ten-thirty and whenever I fell asleep. Such long, tossing, fitful, unhappy hours!

In desperation I began reviving a habit I'd had in high school and lost at Penn State: I began reading a chapter in the Bible and praying as I sat in bed with Whiskers crowded comfortingly against me. Maybe, in this way, I could calm my mind enough to sleep.

I began in the book of Philippians where Paul writes about pressing on and realized quite quickly that my father had been right that painful night on the front porch. In my total involvement with Jack, I had forgotten God.

Oh, I went to church every Sunday, sitting shoulder-to-shoulder with Jack. I sang the hymns and praise songs with joy and listened to the pastor with a critical ear. I knew that afterward Jack would want to discuss the service and the sermon, turning things this way and that, sniffing, pawing, looking for flaws like a cat looks for life in the carcass of a caught mouse. But, I was learning with considerable pain, it was Jack I wanted to please, and Jack I wanted to worship, not God. Any joy I felt was in the touch of Jack beside me, not in the presence of God within me.

Dear God, how forgiving are you toward someone who has become as shortsighted as I have been?

Slowly, weeknights in Amhearst became less terrifying, but weekends held their own special horrors.

And so, on that early September Friday night just after my move, I found myself digging through the trash can for Sunday's bulletin, which I had just thrown away in my brief cleaning frenzy. I pulled it out and reread it, my attention drawn to the announcement about the bell clinic. I studied the words a few minutes, uncertain.

There had been a bell choir at Penn State, and I'd always itched to play in it. To my ear, bells sound so beautiful—lyrical and somehow angelic. But I'd never had the nerve to audition at school because of the music majors.

Now I nodded decisively, grabbed my purse and ran before I had a chance to change my mind. Maybe the bell choir wasn't for a marginal musician like me, but at the very least I'd have something to occupy me tonight.

Much to my surprise, there were only about twenty people at the bell clinic, but those who were there were friendly and helpful, especially the woman beside me.

"I'm Maddie Reeder," she said. "And I have no music sense whatsoever. I just love how the bells sound."

I had found a friend, though her musical abilities weren't quite as bad as she indicated. And she could laugh at herself, a trait I appreciated.

As usual, it wasn't the notes that gave me trouble; it was the rhythms. I concentrated fiercely, and suddenly two hours were gone.

"Practices are every Thursday," said the man who had introduced himself as Ned Winslow, the church's music director. "You have to be at every practice. It's not like a vocal choir where the others in your section can cover for you when you're absent. If you're not here, your bells aren't played. So it's a commitment." He smiled at those standing before the tables. "How many of you are interested?"

I bravely raised a hand, and so did Maddie Reeder. About half of the others did, too, and the Faith Bell Choir was born. We premiered the first Sunday in October with an incredibly elementary song, but we impressed the socks off the congregation. We were to play the first Sunday of each month and for special occasions like Christmas and Easter.

By this December Thursday night, I felt I had acquired a few friends as I hung my coat and greeted the other ringers. We were a club, a group who shared a common cause, common experiences and common jokes. I belonged here.

I slipped on a pair of canvas gardening gloves and lifted two shiny brass bells from their red velvet resting places. I carried them carefully to the practice table and laid them down, then returned for two others.

I arranged the B-flat, B, C and C-sharp in an orderly line. On either side of me, people were arranging their bells, ringing them, sorting their music and pulling on their heavy gloves to protect the fold of skin between the thumb and forefinger from the rubbing of ringing the bells.

"All right, folks," said Ned Winslow. "Turn to the piece we'll play with the vocal choir Christmas

Sunday morning. Merry, note that the arrangement wasn't written by someone who knows bells. The C and C-sharp are written in the treble clef as with choral or orchestral music. You will want to transfer them to the bass clef."

I began penciling in the changes and was halfway through the piece when Ned said, "Okay, let's try it. Merry, just do the best you can."

I hit my first clunker about the same time I became conscious of someone entering the room and sitting on the floor near the door.

"C-sharp, folks," yelled Ned.

How does he know that? I wondered. *How can he tell, with all the other notes being played, that it's C-sharp that's missing? Of course, that's why he teaches music and I hit clunkers.*

As I made the necessary transfer of bells, I realized our listener was Curt Carlyle. I hit three clunkers in a row.

"Want a bell, Curt?" Ned asked when we finished the song. "We can always use more ringers."

Curt shook his head. "I'll just listen for a while, if you don't mind."

Ned nodded. "Okay, choir, let's take it from measure fifty-four, treble clef upstems only, on the runs. One-and-two-and-ready-and-play-and…"

I followed along, thankful that I was in the bass clef, which had many fewer runs. Beside me, Maddie muttered to herself as she counted the beats.

"Now, everyone, bells up," Ned said.

My world narrowed to my four notes. I exchanged my Cs and C-sharps at the correct time and only missed two notes the entire piece. I felt pleased with myself as practice ended and I returned my bells to their velvet cases.

I began collecting the thick foam cushions that covered the tables. Other choir members collected music, folded cloth covers and turned tables on their sides to collapse their legs.

Curt worked his way across the room toward me, talking to people as he moved.

"I knew I'd seen you somewhere before," he said, taking the cushions from me. "As soon as I came in and heard the bells, I knew where."

I felt self-conscious in a way I hadn't this morning. Then, I was supposed to interview him, and talking was my job. Now, he looked very large and somewhat overwhelming, his vitality directed at me, not his work.

"I take it you go to church here," I said. Now there was a piece of sharp deduction.

"From a little tyke," Maddie said as she walked past with an armful of music notebooks. "He used to lob spitballs at me in Sunday school."

"Only to pay you back for the sore shins you always gave me," Curt said.

"I used to kick him every time I saw him," Maddie said. "Just on general principles. I knew I had to or he'd cream me."

"And who would have blamed me?"

"One of these days we're going to marry him off," Maddie said. "Doug and I have been trying for years. But until then, I keep an eye out for prospective candidates." She pretended to study me closely.

Curt shook his head, almost embarrassed. "Get lost, Maddie."

Laughing unrepentantly, she carried the choir note-books to the storage closet.

I slid into my coat. "I would have thought you'd be at City Hall doing last-minute things for your show rather than coming to some meeting at church. Which, by the way, you're missing."

"No meeting," he said. "And I am doing last-minute work for tomorrow. Come with me—I'll show you."

I was conscious of people watching us as we walked out of the practice room together. *Grist for the mill,* I thought. *I bet he's the church's most eligible bachelor.*

"You'll make certain the church is locked?" Ned called after us as he shepherded the rest of the choir out the door before him.

Curt nodded as he touched a switch that illumi-nated another hall. "Don't worry. I'll take care of it."

"It's eerie in here at night," I said as we walked by dark and deserted classrooms. "Too empty."

Curt pulled a key from his pocket and slipped it into the lock on a door marked *Hal Brinkley.*

"Why are we breaking into Pastor Brinkley's office?" I asked, waiting for alarms to clang and whistles to shrill.

"Look on the wall above his desk."

There hung a Curtis Carlyle of a stone springhouse with a wreath on its door and a battered milk can leaning against the lintel. A storm sky of deep, brooding blues and violets was about to tear open and inundate the fragile scene. Stark, barren trees bent before the force of an invisible wind.

"It's wonderful!" I said. "Especially the sky!"

"It's the original of the print I released last year. I'm borrowing it to hang at the show. Maybe it will convince someone to buy a print."

I hesitated. "I've got a question that's sort of awkward," I said, stiff with anxiety about how he would receive it.

He looked at me expectantly.

"Isn't it a bit insensitive or crass or something to have this show at City Hall with Trudy just dead?"

Curt took a deep breath. "I thought the same thing myself, so I called Forbes Raleigh, one of the commissioners. He felt I should go on with things because the invitations were out, the show half-hung, everything moving full bore. He polled the others, and they agreed. To my relief."

"You don't think there will be an emotional backlash?"

"I sure hope not. This show provides well over half my income for the entire year."

I blinked. "You're kidding."

Curt reached behind the painting and eased it from its position. "Spread that popcorn wrap on the floor, will you? And I'm not kidding. I've a lot riding on this weekend."

I helped Curt wrap the picture securely, and we left the office, taking care to turn out the lights and lock the door. We walked down the quiet, shadowy hall. When Curt turned out the hall light, we were in darkness except for the faint red gleam of the emergency light and the weak glow of a streetlight that shone in the parking lot.

Unconsciously I moved closer to Curt.

When we went outside, the bitter wind leaped upon us, pushing its way up sleeves and down collars.

"It feels like your picture looks," I said.

We looked skyward: no stars. Chicago's snowstorm would soon be ours.

I hunched my shoulders against the wind and wished my car were parked in front of the church like Curt's instead of in the side lot where the choir always parked. I looked across the barren expanse of macadam and shivered. It seemed so far from here to there.

"Let me put this picture in the car, and I'll walk you over," Curt said.

Grateful for his thoughtfulness, I nodded and waited. Undoubtedly Jack would have let me go ahead by myself, never thinking to accompany me such a short distance, never understanding that I might feel vulnerable and exposed in the darkness.

As Curt and I walked across the empty, echoing lot, our footfalls were loud in the silence. The light from the streetlamp shone coldly on my car, illuminating the driver's side and casting deep shadows on the passenger's side. Shivering, I thought of the great darkness by the lilac near the driveway at home.

I pulled my glove off and fished in my purse until I found my keys.

"Here. Let me." Curt held out his hand.

"Thanks, but I can do it."

"Of course you can. But let me." He extended his hand farther.

Frowning, I reluctantly gave him the keys. Or I tried to give them to him. Somehow in the exchange, made awkward by his gloves, they fell to the ground.

"Uh-oh." I should have just unlocked the door myself. When was I ever going to stop listening to guys who told me what to do?

"Sorry," Curt said. "I'll get them."

"It's okay. Don't bother," I said.

We both bent to retrieve the keys, gently bumping heads.

Simultaneously a loud sound tore the night, making me jump. I lurched and fell against the car door. Straightening, I stared in disbelief at the small hole in my windshield and the cobwebby cracks that radiated from it.

SIX

I barely had time to register "shot" when Curt, gloves off and on his knees looking for my keys, grabbed the back of my coat and pulled me abruptly down. I landed with a teeth-jarring thud on an uneven surface I realized was his foot. I heard him grunt.

"Someone's shooting!" I squawked. "In a populated neighborhood!"

"Idiot," muttered Curt, pushing me off him.

"What? Me?" I got very defensive. "*You're* the one who yanked me over! I didn't mean to land on you."

"Not you," Curt said impatiently. "Him. Whoever it is."

A second shot fragmented the side window above our heads. Little pieces of glass rained down on us, stinging our faces and getting caught in our hair.

"I thought windows in cars were shatterproof," I said inanely.

"Around to the other side of the car," Curt ordered. "Hurry! We're too exposed here!"

I needed no prompting. The shadows were suddenly a haven.

"And keep down," he ordered, as if I needed to be told.

I tucked my head as low on my shoulders as I could get it and duckwalked around the car past my MERRY license plate.

I don't think I'm too happy at the moment, Sam!

The spot between my shoulder blades itched, and I felt like I had a bull's-eye outlined there in fluorescent paint. "You'd think he was shooting at us on purpose," I hissed, anticipating the killing blow.

I noted that Curt crawled very quickly for a man his size. Of course, he was an athlete, an athlete who might have just saved my life by dropping my keys.

We crouched low in the darkness, hugging the car in the relative safety of the shadows, waiting without breathing to see what would happen next. At least, I waited without breathing until I almost passed out from dizziness. Anxiety can do that to me.

"Breathe, woman," Curt ordered as he pulled out his cell phone. "He won't hear you."

As I inhaled greedily, he flipped the phone open. No comforting screen lit.

"Dial tone?" I asked.

He held the phone to his ear and shook his head. He hit 911 just in case, but the look on his face clearly indicated no ring.

"Did you fall on it?"

He shrugged. "Or I'm out of juice. Either way, we're stuck."

We huddled against the car, listening for some movement, some noise—but heard only silence.

"Where did the shots come from?" I whispered.

"I don't know," Curt said, squinting into the night,

trying to see. He squatted and peered cautiously through the good side window. "I couldn't tell."

"You mean he could be in front or behind or on either side?" My voice squeaked.

Curt nodded. "But I think—"

"Then don't put your head up like that," I yelled, grabbing at him. Caught off balance, he went over with a startled gasp. With his right hand he caught himself just before he slammed into the macadam. His hand slid along the small stones that littered the parking lot, and he hissed in pain.

When he stopped sliding, he lay still, looking at me. "But I think he's over there." He spit out each word individually as he pointed to the far side of the car and beyond with his uninjured hand.

"Are you all right?" I asked, reaching out to pull him back close to the car.

"I'm fine," he said, but I saw him wince as he tried to brush the dirt and little stones from his hand.

"Let me see," I said.

He held out his hand obediently, and little pieces of glass fell from my hair as I bent over, bouncing off his hand. It was too dark for me to see much of anything, so I feathered my fingers gently across his palm and felt the stickiness of blood.

"Here." I pulled a molting tissue from my pocket. "It's the best I can do. Use it as a pressure bandage."

I thought longingly of the neat, clean package of Kleenex in my purse, but the purse had fallen on the other side of the car and been left there with the keys and Curt's gloves. And my cell phone.

"If you don't mind," said Curt, eyeing my tissue

with disgust, "I think I'll use my handkerchief. It won't disintegrate under pressure."

"Is it clean?" I asked.

"Cleaner than that is." And he pointed to my tissue as if it carried plague germs.

I watched with interest as he tried to get his handkerchief out of his right trouser pocket with his uninjured left hand. The man would never be a contortionist. He hadn't the flexibility. After much grunting and twisting, he gave up and gingerly used his right hand, carefully extracting the handkerchief with two fingers.

He struggled with his left hand to make a neat square of the wrinkly white material.

"I don't know," I said as I took it from him and made a neat square of it. "This doesn't look much better than my tissue."

I handed it to him, and he pressed it carefully into place.

I couldn't decide whether he winced theatrically or because he really hurt. Probably he overreacted to pain like Jack did.

"Now what?" I asked, after he had lavished so much time and attention on his hand that he might have been stanching the blood of a gaping, life-threatening wound instead of his piddly scratches.

He shrugged. "I don't know." He rolled onto his stomach and inched forward soldier-style. He tried to peer around the front wheel.

I grabbed at him. "Get back here! What if he's still there and shoots you?"

"Don't worry. He can't see me. And if he hasn't

shot again, he's probably gone. My guess is that he realized he almost hit a couple of innocent people, and he's running before someone reports him or before the cops show up."

Another explosive noise ripped the night. Curt retracted his protruding head like a turtle, and I threw myself flat on the ground, sliding halfway under the car. For a suspended moment neither of us moved. I stopped breathing again.

Then we looked at each other, slightly embarrassed.

"That was just a car door slamming, wasn't it?" I asked.

"Sounded like it."

Somewhere close by, a car's engine caught, revved and drove away.

"Him?" I said.

"Who knows? Probably."

"Probably," I repeated. I was suddenly shaking with cold and fear, and I realized my cheek was resting on a patch of ice. "Well, if he's probably gone…" I sat up, leaning back against the car door and wrapping my arms around my knees. Curt leaned against the car beside me.

"This isn't some accident, you know," I said. "This isn't some guy getting careless during target practice. It's got something to do with Patrick Marten."

"Who's Patrick Marten?"

"He's the dead man I found in my trunk last night."

I felt rather than saw Curt's incredulous reaction.

"There was a dead man in your trunk?"

I nodded. "Don't you read *The News*?"

"Not if I can help it."

I looked at him in surprise. "Why not? It's a good little paper."

"No offense, but I'd rather not talk about it. How'd you get a body in your trunk?"

"I don't know," I answered testily. "Why does everybody think I know?"

"Well, he was in your car."

I glared at him. "Somebody put him there when I wasn't looking, okay? And whoever did it neglected to tell me why."

I put my head on my knees, but I knew Curt was studying me.

"You really *are* Brenda Starr, girl reporter, aren't you?" he said. "Beauty, brains, charm, and you take danger with you wherever you go."

I snorted. "I'm no Brenda. She's a tall, slinky redhead with stars in her eyes. She always gets her story and never gets her man. I'm a short, perky brunette, and the only thing in my eyes is fear. I must admit, though, that I'm in the middle of a story to match any of hers."

"How about the man part?" Curt asked.

"What?"

"The man part. She never gets her man?"

I said nothing for a few minutes. Then I looked at him. "I didn't get my man, either."

Curt stared back, then nodded. "Good."

I frowned at him. He was handsome, personable and very comforting to have along when you're being shot at. But potential romance was the last thing I needed or wanted. Jack still haunted my dreams too frequently.

I changed the subject. "How do we know if it's safe to get up? We can't stay here all night."

"Under normal circumstances, I'd be delighted to spend extended periods of time with you," Curt said. "But you're right about tonight. Too cold."

He stood before I realized what he intended. I grabbed for him again, but he saw me coming.

"Thanks," he said as he dodged my reaching hands, "but I think I'll take my chances up here."

I held my breath for a long minute, and so, I suspect, did he, in spite of his studied nonchalance.

When nothing happened, I began to breathe again.

SEVEN

The police responded quickly to the call from my cell, retrieved from my purse now that the world was safe for democracy once more, and Sergeant Poole and I had the privilege of talking together two nights in a row.

"Well, well, well," he said by way of greeting. "You certainly are hard on cars."

"It's not my car," I said.

"Just like it wasn't your body, right?" His smile took the sting out of his comment.

Curt and I told our stories. I tried to keep it as unexciting as possible, but Curt made the incident sound like an Arnold Schwarzenegger action flick.

Sergeant Poole nodded and made notes, pausing to study the bullet holes in the front windshield and the upholstery to try to establish the angle of entry.

"Could you tell where the shots came from? Or the noise from the car engine that scared you?"

Curt and I looked at each other.

"Over there?" I said, pointing to a field on the south side of church.

"I think so," agreed Curt. "It has to be over there for

the bullets to strike the windshield and the driver's-side window and bury themselves in the seats, doesn't it?"

Sergeant Poole nodded. "Probably." He looked around, but two people from the crime-scene unit were already on their way to the probable shooting site. "By the way, we'll need to keep the car so we can retrieve the bullets and do ballistic studies."

"I figured that," I said sadly.

"You got a way home?" he asked, looking meaningfully at Curt.

"Of course," Curt answered.

Poole nodded approval.

"So that's it? I can go?" It felt so anticlimactic just to leave.

"Yeah," Sergeant Poole said. "What else do you want?"

"Who are you going to put on guard outside her door?" Curt asked.

I looked hopefully at Sergeant Poole.

"Are you kidding?" Poole held his hands out, his craggy brows raised in question. "Do you really think we have extra officers waiting around in case someone needs a keeper?"

Well, I wrote about pared-down police budgets often enough. I understood.

"But someone attempted to shoot her!"

True, and shouldn't that make a difference?

"You sure it was her and not you he was after?" Sergeant Poole asked conversationally.

Curt was so taken aback that all he could do was sputter. I tried not to laugh.

Sergeant Poole seemed to regret his attempt at

humor. "I understand what you're saying and your concern," he said. "I really do. If I were you, I'd be screaming, too. And it's not that I don't think it's a nice idea to have someone sleep on her doorstep. There's just nobody to do it."

He smiled at me. "We're old friends now, Miss Kramer and me. If she needs me, she knows where to reach me." He tipped his head goodbye and turned away. We stared at his back a minute, Curt angry, I lonesome.

Curt touched my arm. "Let's go." We walked to his car where he held the door for me and waited until I locked myself in before he walked around to his side. We drove out of the lot and had barely gone a block when he said, "You can't spend the night alone in your apartment."

"Sure, I can," I said. I listened to the confidence in my voice and wondered where it came from.

"No, you can't. What if he comes back?"

"Again tonight?" I said. "I don't think so."

What I really meant was *I hope not.*

He looked at me skeptically but said nothing.

When we turned down the little alley and pulled into the parking lot beside the lilac, he looked very unhappy.

"It's too isolated back here. You're too vulnerable. You can't stay alone."

"But I've three sets of neighbors," I said as I tried to peer through the lilac, searching for lurking murderers.

He waved his hand toward the dark building. "Big help they'd be. They're all asleep."

I looked at the blank, black windows and admitted what he couldn't know: I'd be in trouble even if they were awake. A retiree who used a cane, an unmarried elementary school teacher who jumped whenever I spoke to her and a teenaged couple still struggling with zits and apparently deaf, to judge by the volume of their music—none would be much help at the best of times.

"Go stay with someone," he said.

"Believe me, I would if I could. But I don't know anyone in Amhearst well enough to call them at one in the morning."

"There's got to be somebody." He seemed to be scanning the roofline for snipers. "Someone from work. Someone from the bell choir. Maddie, maybe."

I shook my head, cursing my mother's careful training in the area of not intruding into another's life unbidden. "I couldn't. I'd feel ridiculous."

"Well, you can't stay here alone."

"Enough already," I said, exasperated. "I have to stay alone. There's no choice, and you're not helping me feel good about it, you know. I'll be fine."

We walked to my front door. He stood close as I fumbled in my bag for my retrieved keys.

"I'll stay," he said. "I'll sleep on the couch."

"No!" I said more emphatically than I meant to and than his suggestion called for. "No. Not that I don't appreciate your concern, but I'll be fine."

I stepped inside and turned to say good-night. I bumped my nose on his chest as he followed me through the door.

"At least let me look around to make sure everything's all right in here."

I watched him with mingled resentment and gratitude as he went from room to room, checking windows, searching closets, even looking under the bed. He was having a wonderful time being in charge. He stopped beside the kitchen phone.

"I'm calling Maddie," he said, and dialed before I had time to protest. We were both disappointed when he hung up without getting an answer.

"You're sure you don't want me to stay?" he asked.

I shook my head. "Think what it would do to your reputation," I said lightly. "To say nothing of mine."

But that wasn't the reason I was saying no. Somewhere in my heart of hearts, he scared me more than the ephemeral killer. Real flesh and blood, *male* flesh and blood, nonpolice, nonofficial male flesh and blood, was more threatening than any number of shots out of the darkness. In fact, I was appalled at how frightened I was of Curt. Jack's wounds went deep.

I watched through my locked storm door as Curt drove away. The smaller his taillights became, the more empty my stomach felt, the more rapidly my heart beat. As soon as the taillights disappeared, I slammed the inside door and locked it. The apartment that had been so cozy and safe not five minutes ago was now cold and threatening.

But the apartment hasn't changed! Not one iota! Get a grip on yourself, Merry!

Would that it were that easy.

Whiskers and I went to bed with all the lights in the apartment on. I knew it ought to be the other way around, that all the lights inside should be off and all the lights outside on. That way I could see any villains lurking, and they couldn't see me.

There were two problems with that little bit of logic. One, the extent of the light outside was that weak-kneed bulb by the lilac and the forty-watt bulb outside my door. All other outside lights were beyond my control, their switches resting within the dark and silent apartments of my neighbors.

And secondly, I was not, for any reason, going to stay alone in a dark room. My imagination was too vivid.

I sat in bed, listening to Whiskers snore and telling myself I wasn't afraid. I opened my Bible and read and reread Matthew 28:20. "And surely I am with you always, to the very end of the age."

I'm not too worried about the end of the age, Lord. But if You could be with me tonight, I'd certainly appreciate it.

I was reading the verse for about the tenth time when a thought flashed across my mind.

God said he'd be with you. Would He lie? Stop asking Him to do what He already promised!

I lay down, and Whiskers moved to my pillow, curling himself against my shoulder.

It's just another experience in the process of pressing on, isn't it, Lord?

I stared at the ceiling and actually felt my eyes growing heavy. I was getting ready to fall asleep!

Then I heard a car come down the alley. I sat straight up, heart whomping in my ears, dislodging Whiskers from his spot on my pillow. He stared at me through slitted eyes, yawned and turned round and round until he was satisfied he was settling into exactly the same indentation from which I had thoughtlessly dislodged him.

I looked at him resentfully. No fear, no concerns, no threats to his life. My fate, on the other hand, appeared debatable enough to be the subject on *Crossfire*. O'Reilly and Geraldo would have an absolute field day. Regis and Kelly would offer tea and sympathy.

I strained to hear. Surely the car would drive on. There could be no reason for it to stop here.

But it didn't drive on. It pulled into our lot.

I forced myself from bed and walked to the living room, feeling like the heroines of all the gothic novels I'd read through the years, the idiots who walked foolishly into danger and death when, if they'd stayed cozily in their beds, they'd have been fine.

I turned out several of the lights and stood in front of the closed drapes, trying to get up the nerve to peek out. Was it peeking that got those imbecilic women into trouble? Or was it running up the tower stairs or down to the deserted beach or into the moldering mausoleum? Surely peeking was safe, especially if one was careful.

After all, there might be no reason to be terrified. It could be someone who belonged in the building coming home extra late. It could be someone who had a new job with strange hours. It could be any number of things.

I straightened my spine, took a deep breath and separated the drapes enough for one eye to peek out. Sure enough, there was an extra car in the lot, parked where mine would be if the police didn't have it.

As I watched, a man climbed out of the front seat and stretched. He was huge!

My heart palpitations would have given a pile driver a run for its money.

The man opened the rear car door and reached inside. He pulled something out and shook it. A piece of material unrolled, dangled, hung limp. He bent and placed it on the rear seat of the car, then climbed in after it.

In the few seconds the dome light was on before the door slammed shut, I got a good look at the face of the man and drew my breath in surprise.

It was Curt!

I let the curtain close, turned all the lights back on, and went thoughtfully to bed.

Curt Carlyle was spending the night in my parking lot, huddled in the backseat of his car in a sleeping bag, all to keep an eye on me. My own private watchman on the wall.

I was very taken with the chivalry of the whole thing, and his kindness was far enough removed from my actual person to induce only gratefulness and a sense of security. I sniffed disdainfully at all those gothic heroines and their solitary struggles. They just didn't know the right people.

I actually slept well for what little remained of the night.

Friday dawned so dreary that I kept all the lights on. It was obvious the snow would be here shortly.

When I pulled the living-room drapes open and looked out the window, Curt was gone. Not certain whether I was more disappointed or relieved, I called the car rental man.

"You need another car, Miss Kramer?" I could hear

the man's disbelief. Well, I understood his reaction. I couldn't believe it, either.

"Yes, I need another car. Can you help me?"

"What happened to the one you rented yesterday because your own car had a body in it and the cops took it? Your car, I mean, not the body." He paused. "Though come to think of it, I guess they took the body, too."

He must have picked up all that information from *The News*. So nice to do business with a loyal reader.

"The police impounded the car I rented from you yesterday because the windshield was shot out."

"What?"

"The police impounded the car I rented from you yesterday because the windshield was shot out," I repeated. "I suspect that, even as we speak, your car is parked next to my car in some police lot somewhere."

There was a short silence. Then, "Do you always have problems like this with cars?"

"Of course not." I hoped I sounded emphatic. "Today's car will be perfectly safe with me."

I wasn't certain whether the noise that sounded in my ear was a snort of disbelief or a muffled sneeze.

I was eating a toasted bagel and wondering how I was going to get today's car when the doorbell rang.

"I thought you might need a ride." Curt filled my little apartment with unbridled energy and aftershave.

"Are you always this awake at seven-fifteen in the morning?" I sounded as resentful as only a night owl can when met with morning enthusiasm.

He grinned. "Used to drive my parents crazy. Mom

and Dad finally made the rule that if I wakened them on Saturday morning, I had to go to bed that evening at the corresponding hour."

"Wake them at seven, go to bed at seven?"

"Right. I got so I could watch cartoons with the volume so low you couldn't hear anything five feet from the set. I can't help it. I love mornings."

"Be careful who you marry," I said. "You'll drive some innocent woman crazy, too."

"Oh, I never watch Saturday-morning cartoons anymore," he said with a smile. "Since I became an adult, I can't handle the violence."

I wondered what the protocol was about thanking vigil keepers for their vigils, especially since he didn't refer to it.

"By the way," I said hesitantly, "thanks for all your help last night."

"You weren't that far out of my way," he answered. "What's twenty minutes?"

"But you came back. I heard you. That's forty minutes."

"Usually." He grinned.

"Sergeant Poole wouldn't like the implications of that. And you must have gone home and come back this morning, too. You're freshly shaved." I hadn't meant to sound so aware of him. The words had just popped out because he smelled so good. "Want a bagel?" I asked quickly.

"No," he said, pulling my coat out of the closet. "We've got to go."

As I drove my second rental off the car lot, the salesman watched me go with the same look my father had had the first time I drove the family car on my own. Both Dad and this man expected disaster.

I got home successfully for Dad, and I fervently prayed I'd do the same for the salesman.

I almost did.

EIGHT

Two nights ago I found a dead man in the trunk of my car.

Last night someone shot out the front windshield of my rental car while I stood beside it.

Life has never been so terrifying.

I wrote on, hoping I could communicate to *The News*'s readers how utterly disconcerted, scared and saddened I was to be so intimately involved in the Patrick Marten story—or that there even was such a thing as the Patrick Marten story.

Later this afternoon I'd visit the Marten family, and tomorrow, Saturday, the day of the young man's funeral, we'd run a front-page profile on Patrick and his premature death.

It occurred to me that I'd better check with Don to see whether he still wanted a detailed piece on Patrick now that we had Trudy's story to deal with. Maybe he'd changed his thinking on space and the number of inches he wanted.

"Marten seems to have been a nice kid," I told him. "I hope we're still giving him plenty of space. His violent cut-off-in-the-prime story will be a good companion to Trudy's cut-off-in-her-prime pieces."

"Mmm," Don said, reading something that looked like a police report as we—I—talked. I didn't think he'd heard a word I said.

I stood, uncertain. Should I go on or should I just go?

But I wanted to write Patrick's story as a major piece. I felt I owed it to Patrick. He was *my* story, *my* concern. Somehow his being in my car made the whole thing personal. I wanted people to know him, and to grieve that such a thing could happen to him.

I decided to wait until Don was ready to talk, and before I knew it, I found myself reading what he was reading.

We left-handed people have all sorts of unusual talents due to the slight scrambling of our circuits that left-handedness often causes—or that causes left-handedness. I'm not sure which way that goes. Reading upside down is just one of my specialties. So is mirror writing, though not mirror reading, at least not without the mirror. I can also write with both hands, though if I get much fancier than my name with my right hand, my penmanship looks like a third-grader's.

On the negative, most of the time I can't tell my right from my left, and I have serious trouble with number sequencing, a fact that makes remembering phone numbers difficult and keeping my checkbook balanced impossible without a calculator.

I stood quietly on the far side of Don's desk and read what proved to be a police report on the manner of Trudy's death.

Apparently she had fallen in the bathroom, perhaps

dizzy from fever as a result of her illness, and struck her head on the side of the tub. She had knocked herself unconscious, and the impact had caused a fractured skull and an epidural hematoma from trauma to the middle meningeal artery located behind the left temple above the ear. The hemorrhage and its attendant pressure, the swelling from the impact itself, and shock had caused her death. This death was ruled an accident.

The tragedy, noted on a Post-it stuck to the bottom of the report, was that had someone been there to help her, she would probably have survived with minimal if any long-term effects.

Wait until Jolene, Miss I-Don't-Want-to-Be-Alone, learned *that*.

When he finished reading, Don rested an elbow on the desk and the palm of his hand on his forehead, his fingers lacing back into his hair. He sat there, eyes closed, the very picture of desolation.

I stood quietly, thinking about poor Trudy, when it dawned on me that nobody likes to have such emotional wrenchings observed by someone he hasn't invited to share the experience. I really should go back to my desk.

I just couldn't figure out how to do it without Don's noticing.

It felt like the time Jack and I were seated at a restaurant some distance from Pittsburgh only to see my recently widowed Aunt Edie ushered to a table two removed from ours. She was out on her first date since Uncle Ted's death—with a close family friend whom we had always thought was happily married to a woman named Molly.

If we stayed, Aunt Edie'd eventually see us, and there'd be trouble. If we left, she'd see us because we'd have to walk right past her table, and there'd be trouble. We'd already ordered our dinner, so we stayed. Why miss our meal if we couldn't avoid the problem, anyway? Still, it had been an excruciating evening, at least for me and Aunt Edie. Jack thought it was quite funny, but Aunt Edie didn't speak to me for over a year, my just punishment for spying, she said. Her punishment was marrying the guy after he divorced Molly.

So I stood by Don's desk, trying to decide what was the best thing to do politically and humanely, and would I be fortunate enough that they'd be the same, and could I manage to accomplish them with a modicum of grace. Then Don looked up and noticed me with a start.

"What do you want, Merry?" he asked gruffly, not happy to see me.

"The profile on Patrick Marten," I said as Jolene walked up with the day's mail and laid Don's on the corner of his desk. "For tomorrow. Should I still do it? How many inches?"

He reached automatically for the envelopes as he said, "Sure. Of course. Why not? Just remember Trudy will get most of the play."

I nodded and got back to my desk as quickly as I could. When Jolene walked by without any mail for me, I grabbed her arm.

"Why's Don so upset over Trudy?" I asked.

"We're all upset over Trudy," Jolene answered.

"Of course everyone's upset," I said. "I know that.

But there's upset and there's upset. Is there something I should know?"

Jolene looked at me without understanding. Then, suddenly, incredulously: "About Don and Trudy? Together? As a couple? Are you crazy? You might as well ask about Trudy and Mac."

"There was something between Trudy and Mac?" Granted he was Amhearst's Casanova, but Trudy? She seemed too classy for a sport like Mac.

"Of course not," Jolene said, her dark eyes sparkling. "And there wasn't anything between Don and her, either."

"Keep your voice down," I hissed, glancing around.

"And why not? They were both single, weren't they?"

"But Don's such a recent widower," Jolene said. Without thinking, she began pulling dead or dying leaves off the philodendron on my desk. She made a neat pile of the crumbling foliage on top of my dictionary, right above the trash basket, which she ignored.

"His wife died over two years ago," I said. "Plenty long enough to get involved with someone else."

"But his wife's death was such a tragedy!"

"People get over it," I said, thinking of Aunt Edie.

"Not Don," she said. "He just loved her to death. Always so kind to her, so caring. Gave her diamonds and flowers all the time. I mean, it was a beautiful marriage." She sighed. "I wanted more than anything for me and Arnie to be like that. I told him about them all the time so's he'd learn."

Uh-oh. Poor Arnie. I scooped up the dead philodendron leaves and dropped them into my basket.

Jolene made little noises like a squeaky fan belt. "I don't know where I went wrong. All's I'd say was stuff like, 'Arnie, Don's taking his wife to the shore for the weekend. Isn't he a nice guy?' And I'd sigh, so's he'd know I wanted to do the same thing. Or, 'Don took a huge bouquet of flowers home tonight. Isn't that the sweetest thing? He sure knows how to make a woman happy.'"

She took such a deep breath that her chest rose a good six inches. Her sigh as she exhaled was probably audible out on Main Street.

"Not that you'd understand, Merry," she said. "You never even got married."

I pulled Jolene's verbal knife from between my shoulder blades, then spoke. "Do you think Arnie might have gotten tired of being compared to Don and found wanting? Or maybe he thought you were telling him that you loved Don, not him?"

"See?" said Jolene, pointing a lethally nailed finger in my face. It sported little snowflakes dancing across its blood-red surface. "You don't understand! It's just like me and Trudy."

"You and Trudy?" I said, not following her. "She didn't understand you, either?"

Jolene looked at me with something like sympathy. "Don't worry if it's too much for you," she said kindly. "Nobody else understands about me and Trudy, either."

I nodded, wondering if I was the only one who saw something significant in that fact.

"I just keep thinking of her and me and how alike we are," Jolene explained as she fluffed and arranged the leaves of my plant.

I looked at Jolene and thought of Trudy. I

imagined that somewhere in the world there were probably two other women more dissimilar. I just didn't happen to know them.

"Jolene, granted you and Trudy are both local and you both graduated from the local high school, but that's about it. You got a job as a secretary at the local paper, married the local jock and you live three blocks from where you grew up. Every night for the duration of your marriage you had dinner with your parents."

"Still do."

I nodded. "And you're separated from your husband and you're twenty-five."

Jolene nodded. "Right."

"Trudy graduated with honors from the University of Pennsylvania and Dickinson Law. She returned to Amhearst in her mid- to late twenties and quickly became a partner in a prestigious law firm, and mayor as of the last election. She served on countless civil boards. She was forty-two, never married, and probably last ate with her parents on a regular basis when she was eighteen."

"See?" Jolene said triumphantly.

I blinked and shook my head.

"We both live—lived—alone," Jolene pronounced with great drama.

"Oh," I said. "Of course. And because you live alone, you're going to fall and crack your head on the tub and die, too."

She nodded solemnly. "Or something."

"Perfectly logical," I said.

Jolene beamed. "I knew you'd finally see it. You're smart."

I smiled graciously at the compliment. "But, Jolene, honey, things happen to people who lived with people, too," I said. "Probably more things if you want the truth. It's relatives that kill you, either by giving you high blood pressure or by shooting you when you forget to take out the garbage."

Jolene shook her head. "I guess you don't understand after all, Merry. Alone is terrible." The last was a whisper as she turned and walked to her desk.

Alone is terrible. I thought about that for a while. Certainly *alone* was hard. And I was lonely. And it could be frightening. But *terrible,* as in the end of the world?

I'd been alone now for over three months, not very long in the scheme of life, but longer than Jolene.

I stared at my keyboard without seeing it as I replayed the past three months. I began shaking my head.

You're wrong, Jolene. Surprisingly, these alone months have been good for me. They haven't been pleasant, not by a long shot, but they've been good for me.

With a jolt I realized that I'd live them again, if I had to, for the benefits I was learning, earning, gaining. I was still a mess in a lot of ways, but I wasn't as big a mess as I had been. No, I was not. I couldn't help smiling.

Sure, I still missed Jack and his excitement; there was no question about that. And weekends were incredibly long. But I didn't think I could ever go back to Jack and the life I'd known. How could I?

How could I, come to think of it, when Jack was no longer asking me?

In fact, I hadn't heard from him by phone or mail for almost a month. I was hurt by this fact, but was I hurt because my heart was being broken still, or because my pride was wounded at his giving up on me so quickly?

I glanced up and noticed Don staring at me, his face dark and angry. He must be still angry from my intrusion into his personal grief earlier. Or he'd seen me talking with Jolene and felt we'd talked too long. Or he'd seen me staring into space as I questioned my life.

I grabbed my coat and tape recorder. I'd go see Curt's setup and I'd go see Mrs. Marten. In my best Scarlett O'Hara tradition, I'd think about Jack tomorrow. And make my boss happy today.

NINE

I walked to the door of the Martens' house with sweaty palms. It was the first time I'd interviewed the family of a murder victim, and I wasn't looking forward to it. I wasn't certain I'd ever grow a shell that allowed me to deal with emotionally charged stories easily—and I wasn't certain I wanted to.

"I'm Merrileigh Kramer from *The News*," I said to the young woman who answered the door. "I believe Mrs. Marten is expecting me."

She nodded. "Come in. I'm Annie Marten Morrell, Pat's sister. Mom's in the kitchen. I'll get her."

Annie left me in the living room with a pair of little boys about six and eight. They were looking at a photo album. Or they were when they weren't staring at me.

"Hi," I said. "Who are you guys?"

"I'm Jonny Morrell, and this is Pete," the older said.

"We're looking at pictures of Uncle Pat," the younger said. "He got killed. Grandmom says that if we look at pictures of him, we'll remember him real good even though we're only little."

"Except we aren't little," clarified Jonny.

"You loved your uncle?" I made it a question, hating myself for interviewing two little kids.

"He was great," Jonny said.

"He took us fishing," Pete said. "Now there's nobody to take us fishing next summer."

"Our dad's a trucker, and he's gone lots and lots," Jonny said. "Uncle Pat called himself our Dad Two." He sketched the number in the air so I'd understand.

Pete stared at the photo album. "I think Uncle Pat loved us more than Daddy does," he whispered.

Jonny thought about that idea for a minute, then shrugged. "He was here more."

"That means he loved us more," said Pete with a child's simple equation for estimating affection. "And he bought us candy."

We three looked at each other from the edges of the immense chasm Patrick Marten's death had ripped in the boys' lives.

Liz Marten and Annie came into the room. Liz had that vulnerable, shocked, infinitely sad expression I had seen before at funerals and viewings. All pretense and protective behavior had been stripped off, scrubbed away, and only pain remained.

"Mrs. Marten," I said, standing. "I'm so sorry."

She nodded her head. "Sit," she said.

I did.

There was an awkward little silence during which I considered without pride my audacity in being here. I took a deep mental breath and began.

"Tell me about Patrick," I said.

"He was a wonderful kid." Liz smiled softly. "I know all mothers who lose children probably say the same thing, even if the kids are in jail for life. But Pat truly was a wonderful kid."

"He taught me how to ride my bike," Jonny said.

"Me, too," Pete said. "And roller-skate. And bat. I was the best batter at T-ball."

"He was going to teach us to drive," Jon said.

Pete nodded. "He promised. He already let me sit in his lap and steer when he backed out of the driveway."

"He let us help him change the oil in our car," Jon said. "He took us to Taggart's and let us get in the pit with him."

"Mom didn't mind too much that we got dirty." Pete rubbed some imaginary oily mess off his sweat-shirt.

Liz smiled. "Pat was one of these kids who's a car junkie, you know? We always had a gutted wreck in the driveway when he was a teenager. He thought going to Taggart's garage every day was like going to heaven."

There was a little silence while she heard what she had said. She closed her eyes in pain.

Annie took her mother's hand and held it, her own eyes sheened with tears.

On the sofa the boys looked back at the album, and suddenly Pete started laughing.

"Grandmom, what happened here? He's all muddy!"

Liz leaned over and looked at the picture Pete was pointing to.

"Remember, Annie?" Liz said. "We went camping for a weekend, and it rained the whole time. Pat was about as old as you, Jonny, and he was so bored! Finally he started sliding down the little bank by our campsite into the stream at the bottom. The ground was so wet that it was a great sliding board. He'd gotten that dirty before we even realized what he was doing. Then your mother started sliding, too."

It was obvious from the boys' faces that the idea of their mother sliding in the mud was beyond comprehension.

"Even Grandpop slid," Annie said with a soft smile.

"Did you slide, too, Grandmom?" Pete asked.

Liz nodded. "But I wouldn't let Grandpop take my picture. And I was never able to get the clothes clean. I had to throw them all out."

I looked at Liz and Annie and the boys. How had such a thing as murder happened to such truly nice people? And why?

Why, God? Weren't you looking?

"Did Pat live here with you and your husband?" I asked.

"Pat's lived with me ever since my husband died a year ago. Before that he had an apartment with a couple of guys." Liz drew a ragged breath and stared at her clasped hands. "This time I'll really be alone."

"We'll be here for you, Mom," Annie said. "You won't be alone."

Liz smiled at Annie, and the three of us knew she would be alone, a wife and mother who had lost her calling.

"Hey, Grandmom, look!" Pete pulled his hand out from under a sofa cushion, clutching a pair of quarters.

Liz put her hand to her mouth as pain rippled her forehead. "Pat always sat at that end of the sofa to watch TV. He was always losing change there, and I kept it in a mug until there was enough to go to dinner.

He and Hannah and I went to Ferretti's about a month ago."

Pete came to Liz, the quarters sitting in his out-stretched palm.

Liz took them, fingering them lovingly because they were one of the last things Pat had touched. Then she put them back in Pete's hand. "One for you and one for your brother," she said. "Uncle Pat would want you to get a candy bar on him."

Pete grinned, stashing one quarter in his pocket and handing the other to Jonny. He didn't even mention that most candy bars were more expensive.

The doorbell rang, and Annie went quickly to answer it.

"Make sure you tell your readers," Liz said, "that murder kills more than the victim. It kills his family and friends, too."

Annie returned with a frail-looking young woman whose pale face had the same stripped look as Liz's.

"Hannah." Liz hugged the girl. "Did you get any sleep?"

Hannah shook her head. "I don't think so."

Annie introduced Hannah to me as Pat's fiancée.

"They were to get married at Christmas," Annie explained.

Interested, I looked at the girl with the listless blue eyes and the fine, limp, light-brown hair. Just two days ago she had been a fiancée. Three weeks from now she was to have been a bride and a wife, someday a mother. Now she had no definition, because a fiancée must have someone to whom she's affianced, and someone who hasn't been a wife can't be a widow. She was that all-purpose person, the mourner, one of the crowd, albeit one with more intense pain.

"Merrileigh Kramer?" she said at my name. A faint spark of interest lit her eyes. "Pat was in your car, wasn't he?"

I nodded, feeling somehow that it was my fault. I barely stopped myself from apologizing.

"Why?" she asked.

I shook my head. "I have no idea."

She nodded and rose, walking to the door.

"Hannah," Liz said. "You're leaving already?"

She paused. "I'll be back."

I rose, too. "Excuse me, Mrs. Marten. I won't be long." And I followed Hannah out of the house.

"Can I ask you a few questions?" I said.

She stopped at the crosswalk and shrugged. "I guess."

I noticed she wouldn't look at me. In fact, she stared over my shoulder with such concentration that I turned to see what she was looking at. There was nothing there except another house with a barren winter lawn, the first beautiful shimmer of falling snow turning it into one of those glass balls you shake.

"How long had you been engaged?" I asked.

"I come here all the time now," she said. "They loved him, too, and they understand. But it hurts too much to stay. So I go away for a while. Then I have to come back. Then I go. Come, go, come. I think I'm driving all of us crazy."

She fell silent, and I was about to repeat my question when she answered it.

"We've been engaged about eight months," she said. "I met him two years ago at a Christmas party.

Well, I really didn't meet him. We'd been in the same high school class, but I hadn't known him except as some guy who was just sort of there. But that night I was mad at my old boyfriend, so I started talking to Pat just to get Andy's goat. Well, I never went back to Andy."

She smiled as she remembered. "You know what our first date was? He took me to church. I'd never thought too much about God before, but Pat thought about Him a lot. I went along with Pat's religious stuff at first just because I liked him so much. Then I found myself believing in Jesus because of my own needs, not because I wanted to impress Pat." She sighed. "I thank God for these past two years. They were the best of my whole life."

Oh, Lord, I found myself praying, *did You have to take this wonderful person from her?*

"We were going to get married at Christmas because that's when we started going together. Romantic and all. Plus the church is already decorated. 'We might as well save any money we can,' he said."

She began blinking rapidly as she tried not to cry. "He was such a special guy. I knew as soon as I started to date him that he was special. He was kind, you know? He loved those little boys—" she waved her hand toward the house and Jonny and Pete "—and he was so gentle with his mom when his dad died. And he loved me."

She gave a great sniff and began rummaging in her shoulder bag for a tissue. Instead, she pulled out a packet stuffed with pictures, credit cards and identification.

"My dad didn't love my mom, but Pat loved me."

She flipped to a pair of pictures and held them out.

I looked at an average-looking guy with brown hair, brown eyes and pleasant smile, holding a mess of fish before him proudly. His jeans and sweatshirt were as ordinary as his face.

"Opening day of fishing season last spring," she said. "He got up and staked his place at four in the morning. He took his sleeping bag so he wouldn't freeze, and he caught more fish than anyone around him. He was so proud."

The second picture was of this young man and Hannah. It was obviously a studio picture, probably taken to celebrate their engagement. In it her eyes shone, her hair was curly and bright and her smile had enough wattage to light Amhearst. She was so beautiful that it looked like a different woman from the girl standing with me in the cold, wintry dimness. I had a stab of realization and a wash of sadness. This *was* a different woman.

"May I borrow these pictures for the paper?" I asked. "I'll be sure they're returned."

She looked at them, then slid loose the one of Pat alone and handed it to me.

"You can use this one, but not the one with me in it. I don't deserve it."

I looked at her blankly. "What?"

"I don't deserve it," she repeated. "It's all my fault. I'm the one who killed him."

TEN

Hannah's words echoed in my ears: *I'm the one who killed him.*

"What?" I stared at the girl. Now I could see that something besides grief had etched the dark blots beneath her eyes. Guilt was consuming her.

"Of course I didn't mean to," she said quickly. "After all, I loved him."

"Are you telling me that you struck him?" Had I stumbled on a common, ordinary, tawdry crime of passion?

"What?" She vibrated with anger, more alive than I'd seen her. "How could you even suggest such a thing!"

"But you said—"

"I said I killed him," she said. "I didn't say I *killed* him."

"Okay," I said, feeling more than slightly bewildered.

She looked around vaguely. "It's snowing. Pat loved the snow."

"But why did you say you killed him?" I asked, trying to keep her focused on the main issue.

"We were going to Vermont for our honeymoon,"

she said. "We thought about the Poconos, but we didn't want one of those places that have heart-shaped tubs and all. Besides, you can't trust it to snow in Pennsylvania. We were going to a cozy B and B he found, and we were going cross-country skiing and snowmobiling and ice-skating. And we were going to lie in front of our own private fireplace at night." She was crying now, large, crystal tears streaming down her cheeks.

I stood with her in the increasing snow because I didn't know what else to do. Finally I repeated, "What did you mean when you said you killed Pat?"

"Andy Gershowitz," she said.

I waited for more, but she seemed to feel she'd said it all.

"Who's Andy Gershowitz?" I asked.

"The guy I went with before Pat." She looked at me with her soggy eyes. "Do you have a Kleenex?"

I rooted in my purse and found the package I hadn't been able to offer Curt last night. She took a tissue and blew her nose. She ignored her tears.

"I've got to go," she said.

"But I need to know more about Andy Gershowitz," I said. "Are you saying he killed Pat?"

"He didn't want me to marry Pat," Hannah answered. And she climbed into her car and drove away.

I watched her go, worried about any drivers she might encounter. She'd never see them through the tears and snow.

I went back into the Martens' house. Liz, Annie and the boys were sitting where I had left them.

"She's gone," I said.

Liz nodded. "She'll be back."

"She seems to blame herself for Pat's death," I said.

Annie nodded. "She's told us."

"And you believe her?"

"Who knows? I do know she's had trouble with some guy."

"Andy Gershowitz?"

Annie nodded. "That's the name. He's harassed her since she began dating Pat."

"Really?" Could someone really be that jealous over pale, wan Hannah? Then I remembered the shining woman in the engagement photo.

"He kept calling her and driving by her house," Annie said. "Often he'd show up wherever she and Pat went for a date. The unnerving part was that he could only have known where they were if he followed them."

I frowned. "He was a stalker?"

"I guess you could say that," Annie said.

"Did she tell the police about him?"

Liz shook her head. "What's to tell? He never really harmed her. He just wanted her back."

"Did he threaten Pat?"

"He called a few times and asked Pat to leave her alone." Liz smiled. "Pat politely said he loved Hannah and would leave her alone only if she asked him to. Which, of course, she didn't. Pat even tried to tell Andy that Jesus loved him."

"Uncle Pat always told everybody that," Pete said.

I smiled and wished I had known Pat.

"She's given his name to the police since the murder, hasn't she?" I asked. If she hadn't, I certainly would. He might be the one stalking me now.

"Grandmom," Pete said. "I'm hungry."

Liz looked at the boy, then at me. "I've got to feed him," she said.

"And I've got to go." I got quickly to my feet. "You have been very gracious to talk with me."

"Just make it very obvious to people that he was wonderful," Pat's mother said fiercely. She left the room, Pete and Jonny trailing her.

Annie walked me to the door, and I went out into a wild, white world. I drove slowly back to the office, my mind whirling like the fat flakes that were already covering lawns and sidewalks. I parked in the small lot behind *The News* building and went inside.

Andy Gershowitz.

The News had nothing on him in the e-files, but Sergeant Poole certainly reacted to the name when I called him.

"How'd you hear of Gershowitz?" he asked.

"I was talking with Patrick's fiancée."

He grunted.

When he said nothing more, I said, "And what does *umph* mean?"

Sergeant Poole grunted again. "Let's just say we're looking for him for questioning."

"That means you think he's the one?"

"That means we want to question him."

"And he's missing?"

"Mmm."

"Since when?"

"Since we're not certain."

"So when was he last seen?"

"We've talked with the guys he ate lunch with Wednesday, the day of the murder, but it seems he never went back to work."

"Where'd he work?"

"Brandywine Steel."

"I know Mittal Steel in Coatesville, but I don't know that company," I said.

"They're a small steel fabricator over in the east end of town. Apparently Gershowitz was a welder there. In fact, he was the welding supervisor."

Suddenly Sergeant Poole sneezed loudly in my ear, and I jumped like I'd been shot at. Again.

"Sorry," he said, sniffing. "I've been out in the cold rain too often recently."

I refrained from pointing out that he had sat in my warm living room drinking coffee while his compatriots secured the crime scene in the rain.

"So this Gershowitz is the one I should be afraid of?" I asked.

Poole sighed again. "I don't know, Miss Kramer. I really don't. Even if Gershowitz is the one who killed Marten, I cannot imagine for the life of me why he would want to hurt you."

I nodded to the phone. "I know exactly what you mean. I can't figure it out, either. But there's got to be a reason, because there's a hole in the windshield of my rental car and no side window at all."

"So what do you know that you aren't telling us?" Sergeant Poole asked.

I frowned. "Believe me, Sergeant, if I knew anything, I'd tell you as quickly as I could."

Sergeant Poole sniffed and swallowed, though he was polite enough to move the phone away from his mouth so it wasn't quite so loud. "Think back to that evening when you picked up your car. Go over it again minute by minute."

"There's nothing to go over," I said. "We drove up to Taggart's. My car was parked outside the garage, waiting as Mr. Taggart and I had agreed. I got out of Jolene's car and into mine. She drove away. I drove away. That's it."

"You didn't see anyone running away or hiding or..."

"No skulkers," I said. "Honest."

"Well, I recommend you don't go out alone until we get this guy safely tucked away." And on that happy note, he disconnected.

Almost immediately the phone rang.

"You ready to come over and see my show? Come right now, and you can see it before the doors open."

"Curt!" I looked at the clock on the wall. It was four-thirty, and I still had the Marten interview to write up. "Give me about an hour and a half, and then I'll walk over."

There was a small silence, and I guessed that he was unhappy, maybe feeling slighted. But I was reading him incorrectly.

"You can't walk over here alone then. It'll be dark, and with the snow the visibility will be very limited. It'll be too dangerous."

"Come on," I said, last night's fear lost here in the bustle and busyness of the office. "It's only across the street to City Hall."

"By way of the back parking lot. I'll come for you," he said.

"You will not," I answered. "You can't walk out on

your own party. I'll be there as soon as I can make it. Now go have fun." I could give orders every bit as well as he could.

I punched off and stared at my keyboard. *Concentrate! Or you'll never get out of here!*

I began to type.

"Murder kills more than the victim. It kills his family and friends too."

With these words Elizabeth Marten, mother of murder victim Patrick Marten, tried to explain the inexplicable pain of the violently bereaved.

I wrote for some time, wrapped in the Martens' pain. Suddenly the emotion of the story got too heavy for me, and I pushed back my chair abruptly.

"Yo, princess, watch it!" Mac Carnuccio said as I caromed into him. He grabbed my chair and rolled me back to my desk.

"I'm sorry, Mac." Here was as big a change of pace as I'd ever find. "Where'd I hit you?"

He laid his hand on his chest. "Right in my heart, beautiful. From the first moment I laid eyes on you."

I grinned at him and shook my head. "You can't help it, can you?"

He grinned back, eyes alight, and asked innocently, "Help what?"

"The flirting," I said. "It's as natural as breathing, isn't it?"

"Been doing it since I was in diapers, or so I've been told."

"And nobody's slapped you down yet?"

"Plenty have, believe me. But most enjoy the fun as much as I do."

I believed him. He had the knack for making a girl feel special, not tawdry, and if you didn't want him to go beyond his outlandish compliments, he sensed it and didn't push.

"Mac," I said, looking around to see how close listening ears might be. I was about to go after information with nothing more than curiosity as an excuse, and I didn't want eavesdroppers. "Do you think Don had anything going with Trudy?"

Mac looked at me incredulously. "Are you kidding? Didn't you see how cool he was yesterday handing out the assignments relating to her? He didn't care a rip about her."

"Didn't you see how messy his desk was and how mussed his hair was? I think he was very upset."

Mac shook his head. "He's a cold fish, just like I said. He keeps people at a distance emotionally. You should have seen him when his wife died. Nothing."

"Jolene thinks Don had a wonderful, storybook marriage, and he couldn't have been involved with Trudy because he's still grieving."

"Maybe they did have a great marriage for all I know. About the grieving?" He shrugged. "Just remember, Merry, we're talking Jolene here. She may be one of the prettiest babes in town, but I wouldn't depend on her great mental acumen. And speaking of the devil…"

With a wave he moved off as Jolene rushed to my desk, eyes wide with shock. She plunked a watering can down on the edge of my desk.

"Oh, Merry! I just found out some terrible news!"

"What, Jolene?" I automatically stood and reached for her hands as her lily of the valley perfume reached out and grabbed me by the throat. I wondered if she had ever heard the word *subtle*.

"I just learned who the body in your car was," she said, gripping my hands back. Her eyes were wide with shock.

"You *just* learned?" I looked at Jolene in wonder. "Don't you read the paper you work for?"

She shook her head. "I don't read anything if I can help it." She giggled self-consciously. "I'm never interested in other people's stories. I guess I'm too wrapped up in my own."

The brazen and unconscious egotism of that comment startled me, and I let go of her hands rather quickly.

Her giggle turned into a little sob. "It was Patsy! I can't believe it! Patsy of all people! I've known Patsy since kindergarten. We always went to the same schools and rode the same school bus and sat near each other because of our names. I *like* Patsy!"

I felt lost. "It was Patrick, not Patsy. Patrick Marten."

"Right," she said. "That's what I said. My maiden name is Luray, so I always sat next to Patsy." She said her name with a heavy *u*, like Southerners say the Luray Caverns. "You know, Jolene Luray and Patsy Marten."

"You do mean Patrick Marten?"

She nodded. "But the kids always called him Patsy. At least the boys did, and some of the girls. I called him Patsy from junior high on."

"Why?" To me Patsy as a man's nickname indicated a shamrock-in-your-face type of Irishness not usually found in America anymore and certainly not in Amhearst. Men named Patsy still lived back on the Auld Sod.

"He wasn't the best athlete, especially as a kid. So they called him Patsy because he played like a girl. But he was so nice!"

I thought of Hannah talking about their plans to go skiing, skating and snowmobiling, and I thought about the picture of Pat with his mess of fish.

"I think he must have been athletic," I said.

She looked at me like I had said something terribly ignorant. "But he couldn't play football or basketball. He didn't like team sports."

I recalled the man on the Board of Education who wanted all the district's monies funneled toward the schools' sports programs instead of the academic ones. Now that I thought about it, the sports he kept mentioning were football and basketball.

"In Amhearst, they're the sports the official jocks play," Jolene explained. "If you're not on one, better yet both, of those teams, you aren't an athlete. Well, maybe if you played soccer or wrestled or ran track. But nothing else."

"Did you know Pat's fiancée?" I asked.

Jolene shook her head. "I didn't even know he was engaged. I haven't seen him in years. Probably some little mousy girl."

"Hannah Albright."

"Hannah Albright?" Jolene stared, amazed. "Are you sure? Beautiful? Perky? Head cheerleader?"

I shrugged. "I guess. I mean, how many Hannah Albrights can there be in Amhearst?"

"But she's always gone with Andy Gershowitz."

I looked at Jolene with interest. Who would have thought I'd find my own private information pipeline right here in the office.

"Tell me about Andy," I said, pulling Edie Whatley's empty chair over for Jolene. She sat down absentmindedly.

"Now Andy was a true jock. Football. Basketball. Track. That's why he and Hannah were such a perfect couple."

"The jock and the cheerleader?"

Jolene nodded. "And he's so handsome and she's so pretty."

"Well, at the moment, she's looking fairly un-pretty, and he's wanted by the police."

She didn't seem too interested in that last piece of news. "You're serious that Hannah was engaged to Patsy?"

I nodded. "They were supposed to get married in a couple of weeks at Christmastime. Needless to say, she's very broken up about his death."

"Why in the world did she pick Patsy instead of Andy?" Jolene looked at me with her wide eyes wider than usual. It was obvious that she was genuinely confused. The answer seemed just as obvious, at least to me.

"Maybe you answered your own question when you said how nice Pat was."

"Yeah, but he was so religious! He never cheated on tests and he never got drunk and he never made lewd remarks to the girls."

"And that's bad? Remember, you *liked* the guy."

"Well, he could always make you laugh. He was fun even if he wasn't fun, if you know what I mean."

I nodded, somewhat disconcerted that she and I were communicating on an intuitive level.

"Now Andy," she said. She reached for the cascading baby's tears on Edie's desk, transferred it to mine and began automatically pruning it with her nails. "He had a foul temper. He got so mad at this guy named Mark back when we were seniors that he ran him off the road. Wrecked Mark's father's new car and put Mark in the hospital."

"Was Mark okay?" I asked.

"Oh, yeah," Jolene said with a wave of her hand. "He still limps a little bit, but not so's you'd notice much. He married a real pretty girl he met at college, so he's doing okay. Andy had to pay a huge fine because of the accident—which I think his father paid for him—and he got a suspended sentence. It was the first time he'd had an actual run-in with the law, though I think there were a couple of times when his father bought off people who could have filed complaints with the police. Oh, and he lost his license for a while, too. Not that it stopped him from driving."

And this was the guy she had thought was such a perfect match for Hannah. "What did this Mark do that made Andy so mad?"

Jolene thought for a moment, hands suspended over the plant, then nodded as memory returned. "You're not going to believe this, but he made a pass at Hannah."

"Really." How interesting.

Jolene nodded. "Really. I wonder if Arnie will beat

up the first guy who asks me out?" She shivered daintily and returned the baby's tears to Edie's desk. She seemed to like that possibility.

"So Andy could be violent enough to hit Pat over the head?" I asked, returning the conversation to its track.

Jolene nodded. "Oh, yeah. Maybe he didn't plan to kill him beforehand, like premeditated, you know, but he certainly could have gotten mad enough to hit him on the spot."

"How about shooting at me?"

Jolene looked at me with real confusion. "But why would he do that? You didn't know Hannah or Patsy. And you keep saying you didn't see anything at Taggart's." She turned suddenly sly. "Unless you're holding back, hoping for an even bigger story?"

I sighed. If Jolene, one of the great intellects of the universe, thought I was playing games, why wouldn't Andy Gershowitz think the same thing?

Suddenly she looked alarmed. "You know," she said slowly, and I could almost hear her new idea unfolding, *crinkle, crinkle,* like tissue wrapping paper. *And it's bound to be about as substantive,* I thought unkindly.

Her hands shook as she reached out and grabbed my arm. "I was with you when you got Patsy. What if Andy decides I know something, too? What if he decides to shoot me?"

"I don't think you need to worry, Jolene," I said. "He probably doesn't even know you're involved. Which you really aren't."

"Argh! I hate living alone! It's so dangerous!"

"You'll be fine," I said soothingly.

"Hah!" she said. "You're a fine one to talk with all

the things that have been happening to you. Besides, you've never been married, so you don't understand lonely. You've never had anyone care for you. You've never been protected. You've never been—" She paused, searching for the right word to nail my marital coffin more firmly closed than ever. "Cherished," she said all soft and breathy, sounding just like Marilyn Monroe. "Arnie cherishes me."

I sighed. A husband who was separated from his wife didn't sound all that cherishing to me, but she was right in one respect. I didn't know cherishing. Whatever Jack had felt for me, it wasn't cherishing.

"Arnie and I may be separated, but he still cherishes me," she said, just like she'd read my mind. Twice in one conversation we'd understood each other, a frightening idea. "I just know he does," she continued. "I'm going home right now and calling Arnie to come protect me." She grabbed her coat and swathed herself in layers of black leather and faux fur.

"You'd actually miss dinner with your mom?" I said, thinking that history was about to be made.

She stopped at this thought, glove half-on. "Well, I'd actually be safer at my parents', wouldn't I? More people. And when it's time to go home, I'll make my father take me. Or I'll make Arnie come and get me. Yeah—I'll make Arnie come for me. No Andy's going to shoot me."

"Where do you live, Jolene?" I asked. It just occurred to me that I'd assumed she was living with her parents since the separation.

"Those new condos over by the old Greeley farm south of town."

I stared at her in amazement. They were gorgeous, all brick and beautifully landscaped, and they cost at least $250,000 each. Arnie must be doing pretty well. Or Jolene's father. She certainly wasn't making enough money at *The News* to buy a place like that.

I watched her scurry out into the storm, shook my head to clear it and turned back to my flat screen. I wrote a while longer, praying that the love and anguish of Liz and Hannah, Annie and the two boys would reach out from the page and grip people's hearts. When I finished, I was spent.

I went to the coffee machine, poured the dregs into my mug and carried it back to my desk. I reread my copy, made some adjustments and pushed the button to send the finished product to Don. Not that he was there to receive it. I'd been vaguely aware of him leaving as I finished up my piece. But it'd be there for him to retrieve and edit whenever he wanted. Ah, the joys of modern technology.

I glanced at the clock. Five forty-five. I'd finished more quickly than I'd expected, especially taking into account the Jolene interlude. It was time to go to City Hall.

I pulled on my coat and wound my scarf around my neck one and a half times, tucking the ends into my coat front. Then I put on my wool tam, turned up my collar and yanked on my gloves. I was glad I'd worn my boots, though the spike heels and the suede wouldn't do well in the snow. Still, I ought to be able to make the trek through the parking lot, across the street and up the long walk to the old mansion that served as City Hall without too much difficulty.

When I walked outside, I was surprised at how thick the snow was, both on the ground and tumbling out of the sky. I looked at the light that was supposed to illuminate the parking lot, but the swirling snow reduced it to a mere halo, a ten-watt bulb taking on a gymnasium.

The one thing I've always liked about a heavy snowfall is the way it blocks all sound. Standing at the edge of *The News*'s back stoop, I listened—and I heard nothing, absolutely nothing. I knew that not far away was a road and across that road was a busy City Hall with lights and people and noise. But I could see and hear nothing but the soft whisper of little wisps of frozen water. I turned my face up and stuck out my tongue.

I jumped as an impudent flake found its way into the minuscule opening between my scarf and my neck. So cold!

As I plowed through the snow, I marveled at this amount falling so early in the season. What would February and March, the notorious snow months, be like? As I pulled even with my rental car, I had a thought: did a window scraper come with the vehicle or would I be wiping snow away with my sleeves, freezing my arms and hands in the process?

Curious, I opened the right front door and took a quick peek at the floor and in the glove compartment. No scraper. I made a sort of *harrumph* noise. Just because I had ruined one of his cars was no reason for the rental man to give poor service. I pushed down the lock and shut the door with a muted slam and backed out between the cars. Maybe there was something I could use in the trunk.

I slid the key in the lock and only hesitated a minute. After all, what were the odds of finding two bodies in your trunk within a week? I turned the key and the lid popped up on an empty trunk. Completely empty. No bodies. No snow scrapers.

I reached up to pull the lid shut. But before I even touched it, there was a sudden pressure on my throat so unexpected and so violent that I couldn't defend myself.

ELEVEN

I grabbed at my throat, trying to pull away whatever was choking me. But through my thick gloves, I could find nothing to grasp. All I knew was that I was being strangled, and that in an amazingly short amount of time, I was seeing the traditional stars—red, they were—as well as whirls and flashes behind my eyelids.

Something that felt like a knee was pressing into the base of my spine, bending me backward at the same time it pushed me forward and into the pressure around my neck. Once again my face was turned up to the falling snow, but this time in fear and pain.

Andy Gershowitz? But why?

I flailed about, tearing at my neck, but all I seemed to do was pull my own scarf out of my coat. My legs could no longer hold me, and I fell to my knees in the snow. The pressure on my neck lessened for an instant to adjust to my new position, but it quickly tightened, if anything with renewed vigor.

God, help!

The peaceful quiet of the snowy night became a roaring waterfall in my ears, and I knew I was losing consciousness. My lungs ached for oxygen, and my head was heavy on my shoulders. Just as I slid into the black waters that preceded terminal sleep, I heard a faint whistling.

Merrily we roll along, roll along, roll along.

Surely celestial choirs sang more spiritual anthems than that!

When I was next aware, I lay on my side, cold and shivering in spite of the burning, searing agony in my throat.

I'm not dead, and I'm not dying! Oh, God, thank you! Thank you!

I gasped great drafts of icy air, each glorious one scorching its way to my lungs. I clawed at the material about my neck, pulling it away as if air on the outside would mean air on the inside. Oh, how wonderful to breathe!

Slowly my need for oxygen leveled off and a more normal inhaling/exhaling replaced my panting. My head ached fiercely, and I realized that I was going to have a sore throat to rival any tonsillectomy patient.

Wait until you see the bruises tomorrow, kid, I told myself. *It'll be turtlenecks for you for the foreseeable future. But at least there is a foreseeable future.*

I was shaking all over, probably more from shock than cold, though the temperature was bitter, frigid, icy, Arctic, Siberian. I caught myself up short before I became a full-fledged thesaurus and looked around the utter blackness. I was—what? Where?

I still wore my coat and scarf, though one end of the scarf was dangling and wet with snow.

"Oh, you wonderful scarf," I said. Actually I whispered, because my throat wasn't working too well. "You and my collar probably saved my life."

I pulled a glove off and reached up; my tam was gone. I reached down and felt dampness on the knees of my slacks. Otherwise I seemed fine. I reached out cautiously in front of me and touched metal. I reached beneath me. Carpeting. I rolled onto my back and put a hand out. Metal. I tried to think.

Metal, metal, carpeting. And something poking me in the back.

I slid to one side and explored what was beneath me with chilled fingers. More metal with holes here and there. It wasn't until I touched the rubber and followed the circle that I knew what I was touching and where I was.

I was lying on a spare tire in a car trunk.

Would it be worse to open your trunk and have a live person go *Boo!* in your face, or to find a Patrick? Either way, someone had better open this particular trunk soon!

I made myself lie still and listen instead of screaming and beating the trunk lid as I wanted. Maybe I could hear something that would give me a clue as to where I was or what was happening. Moments passed and I could neither hear nor feel any driving motion. I concluded I wasn't being taken anywhere, at least not at the moment.

"Help!" I yelled. "Is anyone there?" I yelled as loudly as I could—which wasn't very loud considering the condition of my throat. Even so, my voice bounced back at me in the enclosed space, loud and frightening. "Help! Help!"

Nothing happened, and I remembered with an

almost nostalgic sadness how I had enjoyed the sound-deadening effect of the snow. A violent shiver shook me, then another. I had to get out of this cold, and soon. Between the shock and the chill itself, I'd be in bad shape in no time.

Dear God, I need You again!

And once again I heard the faint whistling: *Merrily we roll along, roll along, roll along.*

Angels again?

The whistling got louder, and I realized I was hearing a real person, close by.

"Help!" I screamed as loudly as my throat would let me. "Help!" I banged on the trunk lid with both fists.

The whistling stopped and a voice said tentatively, "Merry?"

"Yes, yes," I screamed. "It's me!"

"Where are you?"

I recognized Curt's voice and started to cry. "Here," I blubbered. "In the car trunk." And I banged my fists some more. I even kicked a few times for good measure.

"Okay," he yelled, and banged back at me, his fists mere inches but a whole world from me. "We'll get you out."

"Royal we or literal we?" I sobbed inanely.

"What?" he called. "I can't hear you! Are you hurt?"

"I'm fine," I said, but it was a mere whisper.

"Merry!" His voice was urgent. "Are you hurt? What happened?" I could feel him pushing and tugging at the trunk lid, the whole car shaking under his assault.

"Aren't the keys in the lock?" I called. I could see them clearly in my mind, dangling there just as other keys had done that other night. But of course they weren't there, or Curt would use them.

"No keys," Curt said. "Let me try to pull the backseat down from inside the car and get you out that way."

"Don't bother. The car's locked." I sighed. If I froze to death before they got me out of here, it would be Dad's fault for making me so paranoid about evil men lurking behind the driver's seat, intent on mayhem and murder.

As Curt began tugging on the door handles, the car rocked beneath me like a mechanical bull. Finally he stopped.

"I'm going to have to call the police to get you out. Will you be okay until I get back? You're not bleeding in there or anything, are you?"

I tried to remember if my attacker had done anything but try to strangle me. "I don't think I'm bleeding. He just tried to choke me."

I heard an unintelligible explosion from Curt at that news.

The few minutes he was gone to seek help were an eternity. I shivered and prayed and repeated, "I will trust in the Lord and not be afraid" over and over. When I finally heard Curt call my name, I felt my whole body relax. When I heard Sergeant Poole's voice call out to me, I felt like the Old West settlers when the cavalry arrived in the nick of time to save them from the marauders.

The police quickly popped the trunk lock. Arms reached in and helped me out, passing me from person to person until Curt had his arms around me.

"You're all right?" It was as much statement as question, and the concern in his voice was balm to my spirit.

"He tried to strangle me!" I said as my knees folded under me. I grabbed on to Curt's lapels so I wouldn't land in the snow again.

"Here," Curt said, and scooped me up. He carried me to the back door of *The News,* pulled the door open and tramped in, Sergeant Poole following behind.

The warm air hit me, and I started shivering convulsively, burrowing against Curt for any heat he might provide. His arms tightened, and I felt an overwhelming and surprising desire to collapse in gut-wrenching sobs.

Why did I want to cry after the crisis was over? Of course, crying after was better than crying during, at least from the viewpoint of clear thinking when needed. Still, everything was fine now. It was smile time. I sniffed bravely and swallowed my tears.

"You need a doctor," Curt said.

"N-no," I said. "A cup of hot coffee."

He looked down at me, and I suddenly felt incredibly awkward snuggled against him with his one arm around my back and his other under my knees. I pulled away and said rather stiffly, "You can put me down now. I'm okay."

He made no move to release me. "Are you sure?"

"Please," I whispered.

I was shaky on my pins, but by sheer willpower I was able to lead the way to my desk. I kept my chin high with the hope that the tears of reaction might not flow if I acted like I was in control of myself. I arrived at my desk not a moment too soon. My collapse into my chair was not very ladylike, but I hadn't cried and I hadn't fallen.

"Merry!" It was Don, hurrying over from his desk. I could see his face as he came toward me and his back in the reflection in the huge window, now a black mirror, by his desk. It was a disorienting double image.

"Andy Gershowitz tried to strangle me." I blinked like mad as tears threatened again.

"What? When? Where?"

All he needed were *who?* and *why?* and he'd have a story, I thought, but of course he knew who. It was *why* we needed to figure out. "In the parking lot. Just now."

"Don," Curt said, "how could you have let her go out alone knowing what she's been through and the danger she's in?" There was a sharpness in his voice that made Sergeant Poole and me stare at him in surprise.

Don looked coolly at Curt. "I wasn't here when she left."

The two men eyed each other for a minute, something I didn't understand vibrating between them.

"Coffee," I said to break the tension. "I need a cup of coffee." The hiccuppy catch in my voice wasn't due to my dramatic acting prowess.

Don blinked first. "I'll get it for you."

As he walked to the now full coffeemaker, I turned to Curt. "You're missing your show."

He made a dismissive gesture.

"No, no," I said. "It's very important. I want you to go back there."

He shook his head. "Not until I know you're all right."

"I'm fine," I said. And I was. The familiarity of the office, the warmth of the room and the comfort of three men standing around me was combining to make me feel safe. I didn't even want to cry anymore.

"Curt, I'm serious," I said. "Go back to your show. This is a once-a-year evening, and you must be there."

Don placed my coffee on my desk. I sniffed appreciatively and watched the steam curl. My hand hardly shook as I grasped the handle and lifted the mug. I took a little swallow. It hurt. I took another. It hurt, too, but the hot liquid was just what I needed.

"Sergeant Poole," Curt said, "if I go back to City Hall, will you bring Merry over when you're done talking with her?"

"Sure," he said. "No problem. I have to go that way anyway to get back to the police station."

Curt leaned over me and took my hand. "Are you sure you're okay? Do you want to go to the doctor's or the hospital?"

I shook my head. "Please, no."

He leaned down, kissed my cheek and was gone.

I couldn't decide whether I felt relieved or diminished with his leaving. All I knew for sure was that he made me confused and afraid. He was too real, too big, too everything. But he cared. He truly cared, and that was probably the most scary part.

I took a deep breath and turned to Sergeant Poole, who was watching me with a slightly sarcastic grin. I smiled sweetly and proceeded to make him very unhappy.

"I'm sorry. I didn't see anything.

"I'm sorry. I didn't hear anything.

"I'm sorry. I don't know what happened to the keys."

We were finished with our conversation, mostly because I had so little to tell him, when his beeper went off. He looked at it, then borrowed my phone. He stood quickly, unconsciously shifting his gun.

He barely had the phone down before he was in his coat. "I've got to go. Trouble at the Friendship Project."

I nodded, thinking of the darkness out there and Andy Gershowitz.

"You don't have to worry," he said quickly, reading my face. "You really don't. We're looking for him, and he can't hide forever. Because of tonight, we know he's still in town."

I must have looked unconvinced. After all, they had been looking for him when he grabbed me in the parking lot.

"Eldredge," Sergeant Poole called over his shoulder as he rushed to the back door. "Escort her to City Hall. If she goes out alone or if anything happens to her, I'll hold you personally accountable." He pointed a finger at Don and was gone.

"When you're ready," Don said to me.

"Thanks, Don." I smiled and stood. I needed the ladies' room badly. My jelly legs barely got me there and back. When I returned, Don was pulling on his coat.

"Not yet," I said, sinking into my chair. "My legs won't hold me that far yet. Let me write a piece about the attack for tomorrow's paper. It'll get me mad, and it'll give my tibia and fibula a chance to recalcify."

Don nodded, hung up his coat and returned to his desk.

Last night he tried to strangle me. Two nights ago he tried to shoot me. And three nights ago he put a dead man in my car trunk.

Why me?

Previously, whenever catastrophe struck and I asked, "Why me?" I always followed that question with, "Well, why not me?" The world is full of pain and sorrow, and I expect to suffer my share.

But now I honestly ask, "Why me?"

Why does someone want to kill me? Why has he shot at me and tried to strangle me? Is it because I found the body of Patrick Marten? But all I did was find Patrick. I didn't see who put him there. I didn't see the crime committed. All I did was open my trunk and find what remained of a man who by all reports was a wonderful person.

So, why me?

TWELVE

Don accompanied me to City Hall as requested, but it was a stilted and somehow uncomfortable walk. Not that Don said anything wrong or critical. He was just distant and formal, almost like we'd never met and he wanted to keep it that way.

"Aren't you coming in?" I said when we reached the front door.

"Nope," he said, shaking his head. Snow dusted his hair and the shoulders of his navy coat and sat in the folds of his meticulously arranged scarf. "I've got stuff to do."

I got the strong impression that getting away from me was at the top of his to-do list.

I watched him walk away in the falling snow, puzzled. I hate it when I don't know what's going on, not just because I'm a nosy newspaper person, but because I hate to step into sensitive areas when a little information would prevent it. And there was definitely something sensitive between Curt and Don and something odd in Don's recent attitude toward me.

With a shrug, I turned and entered City Hall, a wonderful old mansion dearly loved by everyone who didn't have to work in it with its poor heat and poorer lighting. But its wooden paneling and balustrades, its carved wainscoting and dramatic staircase made a lovely setting for an art show.

The Brennan Room itself was really a large foyer rather than an actual room, and the great chandelier (turned off most of the time for economic reasons) shed a warm and sufficient glow over the gathering.

People milled around, talking with each other and looking at the pictures hung all around the walls and on fabric partitions scattered throughout the room. I recognized several people from church and some from local city government, but the majority were strangers to me. Frankly, I was surprised to see so many here with the weather so terrible.

In the far corner, a duo played classical music on a piano and a flute, their sweet sound a soothing background to the murmur of scores of conversations. A table with a snow-white cloth and a Christmas centerpiece held frothy red punch, cookies, crackers and cheeses.

Spotting Maddie and Doug Reeder coming in the door, I waved and grinned. I always grinned when I saw them because they looked so incongruous together. Doug was at least six and a half feet tall and as thin as he was tall. Maddie was a little above five feet, not really overweight, but not starving, either.

She raised her hand, her wave to me an empty-handed ringing of her E bell. She said something to Doug, who bent down, way down, and gave her a peck on the cheek. Then she worked her way to me through the maze of people while he veered off toward Curt.

I indicated the room, the people and the pictures. "I had no idea it'd be this big a deal. I'm impressed."

Maddie nodded. "Local boy makes good and all that. What's the matter with your voice? Getting a cold?"

"I sound that bad?"

"I'm sure people will still talk to you," she said kindly, "but you do sound sort of froggy. Like you're about to cough in everyone's face."

"I promise not to do that," I said. "And I'm fine. No cold. I'll tell you all about it later."

"What?" she said, grabbing my hand. "Tell me now. When it comes to information, I'm into instant gratification."

I hesitated and she said, "What? What? Did Curt rescue you again?"

"Again?" I raised my eyebrow. "Did he rescue me before? I don't think so. We were equally involved. We both hid under the car."

Maddie shrugged, her long hair rising and falling with her shoulders. "If you say so."

"I do." I smiled. "We tried to call you about one o'clock last night so I could stay at your place. Curt didn't want me to be alone. He didn't think it was safe." I paused but honesty compelled me to add, "I didn't like the idea much, either."

"I should say not. And we weren't home." Maddie's face showed her chagrin.

"Hey, you didn't know I'd need you. It's okay."

"But I feel so bad. Doug had to see a client early this morning in the town where his mother lives. It's about an hour from here. We drove up last night after bell practice, and I spent the day with Mom while he attended to business. We just got back a few minutes ago. I barely had time to comb my hair and check *The News* for the latest about your body. I couldn't believe it when I read about the shooting."

"It's *not* my body," I said.

Maddie shrugged. "It was in your car."

I didn't think she could hear the gnashing of my teeth. I hoped not, anyway. It would probably be considered impolite.

"So where did you stay last night?" Maddie asked.

"In my apartment."

"Alone?"

"Of course alone."

"I'm surprised Curt let you."

"He didn't want to. He tried everything he could think of to prevent it."

"Sounds like him."

"Is he always so—" I hesitated, looking for the right word.

"Pushy? Intense? Forceful?" Maddie grinned. "Yes, he is. Why do you suppose I spent all that time kicking him in the shins when we were growing up? But he's also a good guy, which is why I'm surprised he let you stay alone last night."

"He really didn't."

"He spent the night at your place? I think I'm even more surprised at that!"

"He spent the night in the parking lot in his car!"

"What?" Maddie's squeal was so loud several heads turned our way. "So he *did* rescue you!" She was obviously enthralled with the idea. She probably read romance novels on the sly.

"Protected me, maybe," I said in the cause of accuracy. "But not rescued."

Maddie looked disappointed, so disappointed that I said, "But he did rescue me today." I told her my trunk story.

She listened with growing horror and reached out to pull my scarf gently aside. The bruises were coming along nicely, if her face was any guide.

"I'm fine," I assured her as I rewrapped the scarf around my throat. "Really."

I don't think she believed me.

"You'll stay at our house tonight, won't you? I'll be insulted if you won't. I'm serious, Merry. You can't be alone another night, and Curt can't keep sleeping in his car."

I nodded. "He's too tall. He'll get permanent curvature of the spine. And thanks. I'd be happy to spend the night at your place."

We started working our way slowly around the exhibit, and I was happy for the distraction from my problems. I was also amazed and very impressed at Curt's work.

"I always thought of watercolors as misty and impressionistic," I said.

"Me, too," agreed Maddie.

There was nothing "soft" about Curt's painting. I looked at the old Chester County stone farmhouse with each of its brown fieldstones cleanly delineated. Beside the house stood snow-laden evergreens dipping beneath their burden. It was precise, a work of drafting as much as a work of art. But it was primarily a play of light and shadows, the white of the paper opposite the greens, grays, blues and violets of subtle shadings.

And it was Chester County. I hadn't lived in this part of Pennsylvania for very long, but driving down Route 82 or through Marshallton or out toward Glenmoore, I had seen just this type of house many times.

"I've seen one or two of Curt's pictures before," I said, looking at an uncharacteristically whimsical study of two geese squawking angrily at each other beside a stream. I could feel the tension Curt wanted me to feel between the serenity of the stream and rolling pastureland and the pique of the birds' stretched necks and angry stances. "But seeing so many at once makes me realize his talent."

We stopped in front of a large painting of a stone barn with a weathered red door. There was a $3000 price listed on the placard beside the painting.

"What's that little red dot on the placard mean?" I asked Maddie.

"Sold."

I glanced around to reconfirm what I already knew. "Then almost all of these are already sold."

Maddie nodded.

"But the doors only opened a little over an hour ago."

"Wonderful, isn't it?" she said.

I looked casually around the room until I found Curt in the center of a group. Everyone was listening attentively to every word he said. He gestured to a picture of a springhouse and said something that made everybody laugh. He nodded at them and turned away, only to be surrounded by another admiring throng.

One word popped to my mind: lionized.

"Do people always respond to him like that?" I asked Maddie. Suddenly, as if he felt my eyes on him, he looked directly at me, and as our eyes met, he smiled. At that moment I had almost as much trouble breathing as I had when Andy had me by the throat.

"Most of the time people don't realize who he is, but at an exhibit he's the star," Maddie said. I heard her dimly through the ringing in my ears.

Curt started to make his way toward me—us—and it was like watching the Red Sea part for him, then close in again behind him. All along his line of progress, people shook his hand and patted his back.

"You made it," he said when he reached us.

I nodded and blurted, "I need to interview you for tomorrow's edition." Maybe if I were all business, he wouldn't know how he affected me until I could figure it out myself.

"All you need to say about me is that I'm pleased with the turnout and the response to my work. I'll introduce you to a couple of people who can give you better quotes."

"Like me," said Maddie. She cleared her throat and pronounced, "I know what I like, and I like a Curtis Carlyle hanging above my mantel—provided, of course, that it doesn't clash with my living room colors."

Curt grimaced. "That last crack is too true."

The evening passed pleasantly and ended earlier than it might have because of the weather, but Curt didn't mind. He had been a success any way you chose to define the term, and he knew it.

It was as the flautist and piano player waved goodbye

to Curt that it hit me that I didn't have a way home. My car keys were somewhere unknown, probably buried under the snow in *The News*'s parking lot.

"What's wrong?" asked Maddie as she struggled with her coat, which Doug was holding for her.

"Can you guys give me a ride home?" I asked.

"Sure," Maddie said as she spun around and glared up at her husband. "Doug, remember I'm not six-six like you! Lower my sleeves to real-people height, please!"

Doug obediently dropped the coat below his waist.

"I've got a better plan," said Curt as he came up to us. "I'll take Merry home and get her overnight things. Then I'll bring her to your house, and she can spend the night with you guys. It's not safe for her to be alone."

"We're way ahead of you, guy," said Maddie, her arms finally planted in her sleeves. "We're already expecting her."

"We are?" said Doug.

"We are," said Maddie.

Doug smiled at me. "I just painted the guest room last week. You're the first to use it."

"Whiskers will be mad," I said. "He hates it when I go out at night."

"So we'll talk to him a lot before we leave," Curt said. "Or better yet, we'll stop and get some food, cook dinner and eat with him. Then we'll go to Maddie and Doug's."

I looked at Maddie and she nodded, obviously pleased with the idea of my having dinner with Curt in such a domestic setting. Subtle she wasn't.

On our way home, Curt and I stopped at the Acme Market, where he insisted on pushing the shopping cart.

"I'm just trying to help," he said as we walked

through the produce section, me trailing beside him like a useless appendage. "You've had a wild evening."

Like pushing the cart will tax my strength and nerves to the limit, I thought ungratefully, but I didn't say anything. I couldn't tell him that the real reason I wanted to push was so I'd have something to hang on to. Somewhere between City Hall and the Acme, my legs had gone spaghetti on me again, but if Curt knew, he'd probably try to put me in the cart's kid seat.

For some reason I thought of Jolene and her comment about Arnie cherishing her. While I didn't think Curt was at the cherishing stage, he was definitely at the caring-for-me stage, and it made me prickly and hostile and nervous.

Why? Why did a nice thing like being cared for make me an emotional basket case?

Because being cared for wasn't something I was used to, at least not by any man except my father? Because a kind if slightly bossy man might cause me to think he was the solution to my loneliness, my uncertainty, my pressing on? Because I might believe he could fix my life for me?

But if I fell for someone just so he could alleviate my pain, I'd be like Jolene, afraid to be alone, terrified of the loneliness. I'd be weak again, or still not strong.

And I would *not* be weak again! I would not! I would be strong!

"How about getting one of those Caesar salad kits?" Curt suggested. "They're fast and tasty, my two criteria for food I have to prepare. And get your hand off the cart. I'm driving."

"I'll put my hand on the cart if I want to," I snapped. "And yes, a Caesar salad sounds good to me, too."

He reached across me and grabbed a bag of romaine, effectively trapping me between the cart and the produce, his arm almost resting on my shoulders. Grinning down at me, he winked, then innocently dropped the lettuce into the cart. He moved on whistling "Merrily We Roll Along" under his breath. Next thing I knew, he'd be telling me it was our song or some such nonsense.

I made a show of studying the tomatoes, waiting for my heart rate and my flushed face to return to normal. I suddenly realized I'd better stop stroking the tomato so intensely, or I'd have to buy it in spite of the fact that it was the equivalent of red wood pulp. I put it down and went after Curt.

I found him in the spaghetti aisle, looking at various bottled sauces. We dickered for a while over which we could both enjoy.

"But I don't like mushrooms," I said.

"How can you have spaghetti sauce without mushrooms?" he said.

"Very easily," I said. "I've been doing it all my life, and I don't want to change tonight."

"And I'm supposed to be chivalrous and give in?"

I nodded. "I've had a wild evening, remember?"

"But you can hardly taste them in the sauce. You'll never even notice them."

"Then we don't need them," I said, grabbing a jar with no mushrooms.

"Then I get to pick the pasta," he said. "Linguini."

"It's too thick! Angel hair."

"Too thin!"

We ended up with thin spaghetti, which I secretly suspected was what we both usually ate, anyway.

We drove home in silence. No radio, no tape, no CD, no talking. Silence. Inside the car I couldn't even hear the silky sound of falling snow. It was wonderful. I put my head back on the headrest and closed my eyes.

I thought about Jack, who was a noise man. Always music or talk or TV. He told me he even went to sleep with the radio on, not tuned to a quiet, soothing, sleepy kind of station, but to a rock station with an obnoxious DJ.

"I don't want to wake up and find it quiet," he said. "I hate quiet." And when he smiled that gorgeous smile, he sounded perfectly reasonable to me. I felt appalled to realize that I had been willing to give up silence for the rest of my life just because Jack's smile made me lose what little common sense I had.

Suddenly I had to sneeze, which I always do in clusters. I felt almost guilty as my five bursts of noise shattered the tranquillity of the car.

"Sorry," I mumbled as I held my throat. Those sneezes hurt!

Curt glanced quickly at me and grinned. "You're forgiven."

And silence descended again.

We pulled into the parking lot beside my house, and I noticed Mr. Jacobs, the landlord, had upped the wattage of the light by the walk a bit. Not that it made much difference tonight. The snowfall effectively undid any good the brighter light might have done.

I climbed out of Curt's car and stepped into snow that slipped up under my slacks and bit my skin above my boots. Mr. Jacobs apparently had his own timetable for shoveling his tenants' parking area, and it had nothing to do with need.

Curt bent into the backseat to collect the groceries, but I plowed through the snow, head down, and learned that Mr. Jacobs felt the same way about sidewalks as parking areas. I sighed. If he were as prompt with shoveling as he was with needed repairs like my dripping kitchen faucet, he was probably planning to wait for a spring thaw to deal with the snow. A thaw was bound to come in a couple of months. Or three or four. I sighed. I'd better go buy a shovel tomorrow.

The lilac tree looked like a giant snowball tonight, and for some reason it was less threatening draped in its white mantle.

When the man stepped out from behind it, I didn't even scream.

"Don't scream," he said, needlessly, I thought, since I wasn't making a sound. "I won't hurt you."

I nodded, finding it amazing that the one time the lilac didn't make me nervous, it was doing exactly what I had feared all the other times.

"I read what you wrote about me," he said.

"What I wrote about you?" I stared at the man. He was young, about my age, and big. Like a football player. Tall. Like a basketball player. He had a handsome face with a strong jaw, and he wore an Amhearst cap. His hands were stuffed in his parka pockets, and a scarf was wrapped about his neck. He was skittish, nervous, and spoke in rushed, short sentences.

"Yeah. What you wrote about me."

I'd only written about one young man recently. That was Patrick. But Mac had written about another guy and his alleged actions. I felt my blood congeal. "You're—" I couldn't make myself say it.

He nodded. "Andy Gershowitz."

Now I screamed.

THIRTEEN

"Don't scream!" Andy begged, looking fearfully over his shoulder. "Please! I won't hurt you! I just want to tell you I didn't do it!"

"Merry!" Curt came thundering from the parking lot, tossing the grocery bag aside as he ran.

Andy took one look at Curt racing toward us, groaned and took off.

Curt grabbed me by the arms and peered into my face. "Are you all right? Did he hurt you?"

I held on, the second time in one night I'd used Curt as my prop against collapse. I wasn't screaming anymore, but I was making little hiccuppy noises that I didn't like. I forced myself to take a deep breath, then another.

"I'm fine," I gasped. "He never touched me."

We turned in unison and stared down the alley just in time to make out a figure as it ran under the street-light at the corner.

"There he goes!" I said in one of those needless, obvious comments I'm given to at times.

"Stay here!" Curt ordered, and raced away, veering left onto Oak Lane after Andy.

"Please, dear God!" I yelled an arrow prayer shot straight from my heart to God's. I couldn't even articulate all the possibilities that crowded my mind, horrors like Andy shooting Curt or a car running them both down because they were too hard to see in the storm.

"Curt! Come back!" I raced after him onto Oak Lane. I peered through the falling snow. Was that someone dashing across the street down in the next block? Andy? Curt?

I ran wobbling on my pencil-slim stilettos, sloshing through the snow like I knew what I was doing and where I was going. After I'd run three blocks, I had enough snow in my ankle boots to build a snowman, I had a stitch in my side that felt jagged enough to pierce the frail covering of skin and spill my innards right there in the snow, and my breath made a steam-locomotive sound like a lullaby. And, most upsetting, I had no idea whatsoever what had happened to either Curt or Andy. They'd simply disappeared, their tracks mingled with those of people out walking their dogs or coming from the bus stop two blocks away or simply out enjoying the first snow of the season.

I turned and trudged back the way I'd come, zinging arrow prayers heavenward the whole time. Inside, I felt a weird hollowness that I guessed was fear, both for me and Curt and also for Andy Gershowitz.

As many times as I'd thought about Andy over the past few hours, he'd been an abstraction. He had shot at me, a very concrete activity. He had tried to strangle me, another quite concrete action. But I'd seen him neither time. I hadn't heard his voice, looked into his face, felt his fear. Now I had. Now he was a person. Now he was real. And I wasn't quite sure what that meant for me emotionally.

I was so intent on my thoughts that I never knew anyone was near me until a hand touched my shoulder.

I jerked wildly, the weird hollowness inside exploding into panic. As I jumped, I hit a patch of ice with one high-heeled boot and went down flat on my back. I wanted to leap to my feet and assume a don't-mess-with-me stance, but I didn't have the energy, either physically or emotionally. Besides, I'd never had don't-mess-with-me lessons. Nice girls from nice Christian families rarely do. Instead I threw my arms up to protect myself from the very man I'd just been feeling somewhat sorry for.

My hands were pulled down, and a large man with glasses and lots of snow in his dark, curly hair was on his knees beside me.

"Are you all right?" Curt asked, clearly distressed at my fall.

I glared, torn between relief and anger that it was him. "You should have called my name," I said as I let him pull me to my feet. "You should have warned me you were there."

"I did call," he said. "Several times. But you were off in some thought world all your own."

"Um," I said. I wasn't about to tell him that part of the reason I didn't hear him was because I was praying for him. He was liable to think the common courtesy of a prayer meant more than it did. "I was thinking about Andy. What happened? Where is he?"

Curt shrugged. "I lost him. I think he ran between

some houses over near Trudy McGilpin's place. But in this weather I can't be certain."

I nodded. "I'm sort of glad you didn't catch him. I mean, what would you have done if you had? And what would he have done?"

Curt laughed. "Good questions, and I haven't the vaguest idea what either answer would have been. I just chased him instinctively." He took my arm as we started walking home. "I guess we'd better call Sergeant Poole."

"Again," I said.

With fingers I was proud to see were barely shaking, I put the key in the door and let us into my apartment. I resisted the urge to turn on all the lights in the place, satisfying myself by making the living room as bright as I could get it.

A blinking Whiskers emerged from the bedroom to see what was going on. I grabbed the animal and hugged him so closely that he began to protest. Burying my face in his neck, I marveled at the comforting sensation of warm animal and soft fur.

Curt hung up his coat and turned to me. He pried the cat from my arms, pulled my coat off and led me to an armchair. Then he pushed me gently down and put Whiskers in my lap.

"I'll be right back," he said.

"Where are you going?" I asked, my heart pounding at the thought of being alone.

"I'm going to get the groceries," he said mildly. "I just hope I didn't break the spaghetti sauce when I dropped the bag."

Whiskers and I stood in the doorway and watched

as he pulled the wet paper bag from the bushes by the walk. The bag disintegrated under his touch, and the groceries tumbled every which way. He dived unerringly at the bottle of sauce and caught it just before it smashed on the sidewalk.

"Spectacular save," I said when he came to the door, bottle in hand. "Even Whiskers was impressed."

When Curt returned with the rest of the groceries, I was on the phone with 911. As I talked, Whiskers stalked me, butting me in the shins in a determined campaign for food.

"Does he do that often?" Curt asked.

I nodded as I listened to the police dispatcher saying he would get my message to Sergeant Poole as quickly as he could.

"Where's his food?" Curt asked.

"Top shelf in the last cabinet," I said as I hung up. "I used to keep it in a bottom cabinet, but he learned how to wrap his paw under the base of the door and pull it open. Then he'd chew through the cat-food bag. It had so many holes that it bled pellets every time I picked it up. Finally I got smart and moved it."

As soon as Whiskers heard the dry rustle of his food, he abandoned my shins and began wrapping himself lovingly around Curt's legs.

"Fickle beast," I said. "I'll be back. I'm going to get warm, dry socks. Want a pair?"

"They'd fit?"

"Does it matter? They'd be dry."

"I'll take a pair. And a towel," he added as melting snow ran from his ringlets down his glasses.

I took Curt a fluffy towel and a pair of my brother,

Sam's, socks that I had confiscated to keep my feet warm at night. Then I took my boots off in the bathroom, dumping the ice and snow in the tub. Staring down at the soaked leather, I lamented the probable loss of my favorite footwear. I also studied my red, chapped ankles, then slathered hand lotion on them, ignoring the stinging. Finally, I slipped on my warmest socks and a pair of sneakers.

While we waited for the water to boil for the pasta, we made the salad and heated the sauce. We baked a roll of Pillsbury French bread to go with our Italian feast.

"He said he didn't do it," I said as I placed my mismatched silverware on the little table in the dining room.

"He said he didn't do what?" Curt asked, carefully folding napkins into neat triangles. "He didn't kill Pat? He didn't shoot at you? He didn't try to strangle you? What?"

I shook my head. "I don't know what he meant. Maybe he didn't do any of it?"

"That's a pretty big jump in logic," said Curt. "Remember that the circumstantial evidence clearly points toward him."

"Just because he used to date Hannah?"

"Along with other things like stalking and disappearing and running." Curt took two glasses from the cupboard and carried them to the table. "Don't automatically jump to his side on this thing, Merry. He could be lying. He probably *is* lying."

"Okay, he probably is, but why is he still hanging around Amhearst? If he did kill Pat, why hasn't he run? Wouldn't you run?"

"That's a hard question to answer," said Curt as he checked the pasta for doneness. "I've never even thought about killing anyone, let alone done it. I don't know how I'd think in those circumstances."

I looked at him, exasperated. "Can't you try to imagine?"

He held out a piece of spaghetti to me. "Is it done yet? And while I don't know if I'd run or not, I certainly don't think I'd stop to talk to the woman I was trying to kill."

"Which brings us back to why was he here tonight? He had to have some reason to speak to me. He never did before. I think he's genuinely upset." I forked pasta onto our plates. "How hungry are you?"

"That's plenty," Curt said, rescuing his plate and ladling on sauce. "Of course he's upset. Wouldn't you be upset if you'd killed one person but kept missing the next target? Do you always bleed for the underdog?"

"My parents say I do. My brother, Sam, says I do. He calls me Marshmallow Merry. I just like to help people."

"It's a wonder you haven't married some poor schlep who needed his hand held, and you thought that was love," he said with a weird sort of kind criticism.

I hoped he thought the flush that rushed up my neck and face was a reflection from the spaghetti sauce.

He grinned at me. "But I must say that however that scenario was thwarted, I'm glad."

I became very intent on pouring my Diet Coke neatly into my glass.

When we finally started to eat, I thought what a poor choice we had made for a first meal together. Nothing revealed weaknesses in manners faster than spaghetti. Flippy ends. Drippy sauce. Spatters on clothes.

I watched to see if Curt was a twirler or a cutter. Recently I had come to wonder about the depth of friendship a twirler can have with a cutter. Jack was a cutter, and that should have been warning enough. I'd been too infatuated to see the handwriting on the wall. *Mene, mene, tekel, uparsin.* You have been weighed in the balance and found wanting, because you are a cutter.

I sighed in relief. Curt was a twirler. That was nice. Curt was nice.

Nice? I could hear Jack say. *Nice? Nice is what you say when you're too polite to tell the truth about a person. Nice means exactly nothing—unless it's that you've got too many manners to say anything unkind.*

Jack is wrong, I thought. *Nice does mean something. It means Curt and the kindness he's shown me.*

We were halfway through dinner before I found the courage to ask the question that was eating at me.

"Why don't you and Don like each other?" I blurted. "I don't understand. You're both such nice guys."

Curt studied his spaghetti very carefully for a full minute without saying anything. Then, ruefully, "I didn't realize it was that obvious."

I nodded. "It's only obvious by comparison. You're so pleasant and polite to everyone else that your antipathy toward him shows."

"Antipathy, eh? Good word." He slathered a piece of French bread with enough butter to raise his cholesterol a good hundred points but said nothing more.

I took the hint. "I'm sorry. I shouldn't have asked."

He shook his head. "I don't mind your asking. Really I don't. I'm just trying to figure out how to answer you. After all, you work for the man."

I nodded and waited, but before he could continue, the doorbell rang.

Sergeant Poole refused my offer of a plate of spaghetti. "I was at McDonald's when I got your call. Just had a Big Mac. Thanks, though."

"How'd things go at the Project?" I asked, referring to the call he'd gotten—was it only hours ago? It felt like weeks—at *The News* office.

"Nothing special. Domestic squabble. Too much liquor." He shrugged. "They'll be fine until tomorrow night."

"Don't you get tired of it all?" I asked.

"Sometimes. But someone's got to hold the line. For some reason, I think that someone's got to be me."

"You feel called to be a cop," I said.

He seemed uncomfortable with that idea. "I don't know about that. Ministers are called. Missionaries are called. Like by God, you know? Me, I just feel I got to hold the line."

There was a moment of silence as we all thought about that. To me it was nothing short of a miracle that a man or woman was willing to hold that line against problems of an evil nature I couldn't even begin to imagine. Ministers and missionaries I understood. They had answers to offer. But a cop risked his life just to hold the line for me and civilization. Amazing and wonderful.

"So," Sergeant Poole said, shaking off the philosophical lapse for what really mattered. "You had a face-to-face with Andy Gershowitz."

I nodded. "But he didn't hurt me. He didn't even touch me. And he said he didn't do it."

Sergeant Poole cocked his head and snorted. "Oh, he did it all right. We've got the weapon, a massive crescent wrench that used to belong to Pat Marten's father. Apparently Pat always used it in memory of his dad." Sergeant Poole shook his head at the irony of such a family piece being used as the weapon. "And it's covered with Gershowitz's fingerprints. Clear as a bell. The possibilities came down late this evening from IAFIS, and the fingerprint man at the Lancaster Barracks made the final match."

I knew the Lancaster Barracks meant the state police, but I was unfamiliar with IAFIS.

"Integrated Automated Fingerprint Identification System," Sergeant Poole explained. "It's an FBI database available to us upon request. It narrows the choice down to about ten, but an officer has to do the final match. We have Gershowitz's prints on file from the time he got in trouble when he was in high school and from a DUI last year, and we have a positive match."

"What a tragedy," I said. "His life's as ruined as Patrick's."

"Merry." He looked at me very seriously. "He's still breathing, which is more than you can say for Patrick. And he's a murderer. Don't feel too sorry for him. Remember he's tried to kill you, too."

"But why would he seek me out tonight?" I said.

"For the same reason he sought you out before," Poole said.

"But he didn't hurt me."

"*This* time. He didn't hurt you this time. He didn't know you had anybody with you, right? You said you came down the walk alone because Curt was getting the food from the backseat."

I nodded. "You're right. Who knows what he would have done if Curt hadn't been there. But I still come back to *why*. Why was he here? And why does he want to kill me?"

"I know you're not going to like this," Poole said, his face apologetic, "but I keep thinking there's something you know that you don't know you know."

I shook my head. "I've gone over that evening in my head so many times. Believe me, there's nothing."

"Want to try a hypnotist?" he asked. "There's a guy in Philadelphia that we could contact."

I shrugged. "Do you think it'll help?"

"Can it hurt?"

I looked at Curt. He spread his hands in a why-not gesture.

"Okay," I said.

Sergeant Poole left soon after, and we finished our dinner. I served Curt a piece of Pepperidge Farm chocolate layer cake and said, "Okay. Tell me about Don."

"If I can have a cup of that coffee I'm smelling."

"It's not Starbucks, but it's not too bad," I said as I poured him a mugful. "Now give."

"My sister, Joan, and I had a great childhood," Curt said. Talk about beginning at the beginning. "Our parents were wonderful—fun, involved in our lives and thoroughly committed to living as Christians should. They held us accountable for chores and behavior and homework, all the old-fashioned things, but we laughed. We laughed a lot." He smiled softly as he spoke.

"Joan brought home various boyfriends through the years, and as her younger brother, I looked them all over and disapproved of them all. Then she brought home Don."

"Don?" I blinked. "Your sister dated Don?"

"My sister married Don."

I thought of Jolene's nattering about Don's wonderful marriage and looked at Curt's unhappy face. Something didn't ring true.

"Joan was in her early twenties when Don came to town to be editor of *The News*. She met him at church and fell hard for him. He was a few years older, but he seemed equally taken with her."

"But you didn't like him any more than the others," I said.

Curt shook his head. "It was more than that. I didn't trust him. I was about twenty, ignorant as only a kid who grows up in a healthy home can be, but I knew something wasn't right. I might have thought it was just me, but Mom and Dad weren't overjoyed, either. I think Joan's wedding day was one of the saddest days of their lives."

"But I've heard such glowing stories about Don's storybook marriage."

Curt stirred his coffee, staring into the miniature vortex. "I know. He was—is—a master at appearances."

"But if Joan was happy…"

Curt nodded. "She was, at least at first. Then the inner glow that she'd always had started to dim. Oh, not all the time, and not enough so that others noticed. But we did, Mom and Dad and I. See, Joan thought that you could just take people as they appeared. She had no guile, and she didn't know how to look for it in others. She thought all men were as nice and kind as our father."

"Or as nice and kind as you," I said, reaching out and putting my hand over his, where it was frozen to the stirring spoon.

He smiled at me, momentarily distracted, and put the spoon down. He drew a deep breath. "But Don is not nice or kind."

I thought about that. Don had never been unkind to me, despite his distance and distraction since Trudy's death, nor had I seen him be unkind to anyone at the paper. Oh, he worked us all hard, and he sometimes made guys like Mac Carnuccio angry, but that was no different than countless bosses who also made fine husbands. And Don didn't ask anything from us that he wasn't willing to do himself.

"Sounds ridiculous, doesn't it?" said Curt.

"It does," I said. "But I can see you're convinced."

Curt looked at me somberly. "I've said more than I should. I'm not being fair to you, putting you in this position, asking you to listen to horrible things about your boss."

I waved his comment aside. "I asked, remember? It's okay."

He shrugged. "Maybe."

"You said Joan met Don at church. That surprises me. I've never seen him there."

"He hasn't come since Joan's death. He says he's

mad at God for taking her, but he wasn't coming very often before she died. I think he felt church was a good place to join when he first came to Amhearst, sort of like the country club or a lodge, somewhere you'd meet people and establish yourself in a new community." He looked at me. "Sounds cynical, doesn't it? And judgmental."

I nodded. But there was something about Curt that made me give weight to his words. Of course, I was the one who wanted to think Andy Gershowitz innocent, a fact that shouldn't make me feel too confident in the character-analysis department.

"I don't know, Merry!" I jumped as Curt suddenly erupted from his chair and began pacing. "I've never said this to any person before tonight, and it's been gnawing at me for years, but I think Don abused Joan."

My jaw dropped in absolute surprise.

"I know, I know," he said, looking absolutely miserable. "Sounds unbelievable, doesn't it? Don, Mr. Nice Guy, Mr. Responsible, Mr. Community, Mr. Wonderful Husband. But I've struggled with this for years. And the truth is…well…" He paused, obviously unwilling to go on.

"Well, what?" I prompted, almost wishing he wouldn't continue. "What is it you don't want to say?"

"The truth is," he said quietly, "I honestly think he killed her."

FOURTEEN

I spent a wakeful night in Maddie and Doug's newly painted guest room, tossing restlessly beneath their new teal-and-lavender quilt.

"Go right to bed," Curt had told me when he dropped me off. "You need a good, solid night's sleep."

"I'll probably read or watch TV for a while to unwind," I said.

"But not for too long," he said with that exasperating I-know-what's-best look. "You need a good night's sleep."

And I said snippily to the man who had chased a murderer all over town for me, "Curt, I think I'm old enough to know when I need to go to sleep." And I'd climbed out of his car, pulling my overnight bag behind me.

I finally fell asleep for a few minutes just before the alarm sounded. I pulled myself from bed, feeling punch-drunk and woozy and crabby.

See, Curt? I turned my light out, and a lot of good it did me.

My humor didn't improve when I discovered I'd

forgotten my toothbrush. I went down to breakfast feeling like one of those people in the mouthwash commercials, the ones whose greetings cause everyone else to faint at the halitosis. I didn't say good morning from behind my raised hand, but I felt I should. The upside is that orange juice tastes much better without Crest breath.

Curt picked me up, and I smiled sweetly around the Life Saver I had found in the bottom of my purse. He drove me to the car rental dealer, who blanched when he saw me coming.

"It's okay," I said quickly. "Your car's okay. I just lost the keys."

"I don't think I'll ask how," the man said. "I don't think I want to know."

He was right. "I just dropped them in the snow," I said, and left it at that.

"Now, Merry," Curt said as he dropped me at *The News* with the extra set of car keys clutched in my hand. "Don't wander off by yourself today. Promise?"

I hesitated. He wasn't asking anything unreasonable, especially for the man who had been acting as my keeper. So why were my hackles up?

Ah! He wasn't asking anything. He was telling, and I didn't want any man to tell me what to do, not ever again.

"Merry!" Curt was clearly exasperated by my lack of response. "You've used up several of your nine lives these last few days. Someone's still trying to kill you! Don't take irresponsible risks."

I could feel the stubborn set of my mouth. Who did he think he was? Jack?

"Merry." He placed his hand on my arm. "Don't go anywhere by yourself. I mean it."

"Don't tell me what I can and can't do," I snapped before I realized I was going to.

He looked like I'd had the bad taste to burp out loud in church.

"I just broke up with a guy who always told me what to do," I said. "I'm very sensitive on that topic."

"*Touchy* might be a better word," he said coldly.

"Whatever." I stared stubbornly at him, knowing I was being ridiculous, knowing he was just being nice. Pushy, intense, overwhelming—true—but nice. We stared at each other, the temperature between us as chill as the air.

Finally I said, "I've got to cover both Trudy's and Pat's funerals today. Certainly nothing's going to happen to me in broad daylight among lots of people."

He nodded and smiled. "Okay. My exhibit closes at five. I'll come for you then, and you can watch me tear everything down. You can be in on the really glamorous part of being an artist and help lug paintings and paraphernalia to the car."

I was ready to say, "That sounds fine to me," but he continued. "I mean it, though, when I say just don't go off alone, especially after dark. Now promise me."

I didn't slam the car door, but I came awfully close. And I didn't promise.

By ten I sat in the largest church in Amhearst on one of many wooden chairs hastily placed along the back of the sanctuary to handle the overflow crowd. I felt like a soda left too long uncorked, slowly losing what little fizz I had left. I had to force myself to concentrate on what was going on around me.

Trudy McGilpin's funeral had turned into An Event, Amhearst-style, with state congressional representatives, county commissioners and officeholders from the surrounding towns and townships sitting with local dignitaries in impressive ranks. All these illustrious folks sat directly behind the McGilpin family, who crowded together for comfort. There was no riderless horse with boots turned backward in the stirrups, but the funeral was a decidedly impressive acknowledgment of Trudy's standing in the community.

It was a nice funeral as funerals go. Her brother, Stanton, told little stories about Trudy, the older sister and advice giver. Mr. Grassley, her law partner, told about Trudy, the charming woman, gifted lawyer and wily politician. The mourners laughed several times in a gentle, reverent, I-remember kind of way. A longtime friend from high school sang a couple of songs, and I marveled that she could do so without breaking down. I listened to Dr. Robison, the imposing cleric who led the service. His majestic voice swooped and soared about the sanctuary, by turns somber, then intimate, then full of urgency, his robes billowing with every movement of his arms.

"She's not gone as long as she lives in your heart," he assured, his hand placed on his chest. "She's not gone as long as your memories unreel on the screen of your mind." Hand to head.

I thought that he'd be great in community theater, declaiming Shakespeare like an American Richard Burton.

"She accomplished so much in her short life. Let

her be an example to you of what you can do with dedication and hard work. Be all you can be!" He threw his arms wide at the magnificence of the thought. "It would be the ultimate tribute to Trudy." His voice dropped dramatically to a whisper. "It would make her proud."

Tripe, I thought cynically. *Pure tripe. Lord, when I die, let them say something of more eternal significance at my funeral. Please.*

Suddenly Dr. Robison looked less regal and more human as he said, "She always sat in the tenth pew on the aisle. I'm going to miss her smile every Sunday."

His voice broke, and he had to pause and swallow his grief. In that moment I liked him very much.

Dr. Robison raised his arms for the benediction, and as the congregation bowed, suddenly I could see Don Eldredge. He was seated near the front of the church, head unbowed as he stared straight ahead.

Last night's conversation with Curt leaped to my mind.

"I honestly think he killed her," he had said.

"Curt!" I had cried. "You can't be serious!" It was a foolish comment, but I couldn't help it. It just popped out.

"I wish I weren't," he'd said. He slumped into his chair, all his fierceness gone. "I wish I weren't."

I stared at him in silence while he stared at the floor. I couldn't put together enough coherent thoughts to come up with a reasonable question or comment. Finally I managed, "Do you mean that you think Don killed Joan—as in murder?"

He shook his head. "No. But I think maybe as in

manslaughter. See, she died from hitting her head on the fireplace hearth."

"And you think Don—what?" Obviously he couldn't hit her with the hearth.

"I think Don pushed her. I think she fell as a result of his manhandling her."

"What did he tell the police?"

"He told the police that he came home and found her dead."

"And they believed him?"

"They saw no reason not to believe him."

"Did he have an alibi?"

Curt nodded. "He was at Ferretti's having coffee with one of his cronies."

"Well, then…" I didn't know what to say or think.

"But Joan had this unexplained bruise on her right upper arm," Curt said. "The police think someone grabbed her hard enough to leave the mark, but there's no way to know who that was or when it happened. Just sometime premortem.

"I think Don came home from work, and they got into an argument. He grabbed her arm and shook her, causing her to lose her balance and fall. Or maybe he pushed her away, causing her to lose her balance. It wasn't premeditated. Nobody, including me, thinks that."

I felt a wash of relief. "So it was an accident!"

"Yes. And no. When she fell and struck her head, she hit the area just behind the left temple. If she had hit anywhere else, she'd have had a bad headache, maybe even a fractured skull, but she probably wouldn't have died. As it is, she didn't die immediately. If Don was responsible for her fall, he left her there, and she died because of that desertion."

The anguish in his voice broke my heart.

"I struggle with these facts all the time," Curt said. "I know that, as a Christian, I'm to love my enemy and all that good stuff. And I take those concepts very seriously. So here I am suspecting a man of Joan's death, not a particularly loving thing. And I suspect him with no proof, only my gut feeling, again not particularly loving."

I made some small sound, wanting to be sympathetic and supportive. I hadn't the foggiest idea how I'd feel if someone did something hurtful to my brother, Sam, but I knew it wouldn't be especially loving.

Curt started stirring his coffee again, and I reached out once more to him. This time he dropped the spoon and grasped my hand. I felt like a lifeline he was holding on to for dear life. Maybe I was.

"I find I can leave the situation and its resolution in God's hands if I don't have to be around Don," Curt said. "It's hard for me because I'm a fixer, a problem solver. I like order. I like to have all the answers."

"I've noticed," I said drily.

He gave a weak nod. "But when I see him, I can't act naturally. I find myself dealing with a seething anger that frightens me."

We sat in silence for a while until suddenly he turned my hand over and kissed my palm. I jumped gently at the unexpectedness and the sensation.

"Sorry," I said, blushing. "It tickled."

He grinned halfheartedly, dropped my hand and said, "We'd better clean up and get to Reeders'. Doug will be wanting his beauty sleep."

Hours later I lay in the guest room at Maddie and Doug's and stared at the new floral border, aching on Curt's behalf. I knew what it felt like to be alone in a new town, to feel like I was swinging in the breeze with my usual footing ripped from under me. But I also knew I had pulled the footing loose myself, and I had a loving family waiting back in Pittsburgh if I needed them. Curt was alone as only someone with no living family can be. His parents were dead, killed by a drunk driver, and his only sister had died not long after, perhaps because of deliberate negligence on the part of another.

That, my dear Jolene, is alone. And that is pressing on, in spite of loss and pain and unanswered questions.

I admired Curt, more than I wanted to admit.

But Don—a killer?

I knew that in the vast majority of murders and killings, family members and friends were responsible. I knew that the police knew this far better than I did. They hadn't arrested Don. Had they questioned him? They must have for his alibi to have become known. Besides, they'd be negligent if they hadn't.

But Don? Manslaughter?

Dr. Robison's mighty voice boomed, "Amen!" and I dragged myself back to the business at hand. I had to write about this funeral, after all.

The line for the cemetery was long, long. Had the funeral director tried to observe political protocol in the order of cars in the procession? I imagined there were more than a few in attendance who actually cared who went before them—or more probably whom they went before. Petty people. They deserved to bring up the rear with the press.

It was overcast and cold by the grave, though the KYW weatherman had told me on the way over that things would warm way up by evening. For now, though, the baskets of flowers were already shriveling as they lay on the crusty snow.

The McGilpins sat on folding chairs by the open grave, eyes behind dark glasses. Mr. McGilpin grasped his wife's hand, and Stanton had his arm around her shoulders. How does a mother cope with burying her daughter?

I looked at all the people standing with heads bowed against the nasty wind. What were they thinking? What did they feel?

"I am the resurrection and the life," intoned Dr. Robison. "He that believeth in me, though he were dead, yet shall he live."

Did the McGilpins believe in Jesus? Not simply the historical Jesus, but Jesus, the Son of God who died for their sins? That's where the hope of life after death came from.

"Oh, death, where is thy sting? Oh, grave, where is thy victory?" asked Dr. Robison, who didn't answer the questions. After a short silence, he said, "Into Thy hands we commend her spirit. Amen."

At the *amen,* the funeral director handed carnations to the family and those standing nearest the grave. One by one they walked to the coffin and placed the carnations on the lid. Mrs. McGilpin was led away by her husband and son, her hand pressed against her lips to hold back her sobs. As the rest of the mourners released their flowers, they, too, walked silently to their cars.

Standing to the side, I allowed the mourners to leave, my heart heavy for them. I shivered, and not from the wind wrapping its frigid arms about me or the cold pushing its way up through my boots. I glanced back at the grave.

Don alone still stood there, carnation in hand. He stared at the coffin for a long, unguarded moment. Rarely had I seen such raw pain. A shudder ran through him as he bent down and placed his flower with the others.

Then, instead of straightening, he put out his hand and placed it gently on the coffin in an intensely intimate gesture, as if he were caressing Trudy herself. I felt I was intruding, and I looked away to give him privacy.

So I had been right and Jolene had been wrong. There had been something beyond friendship between Don and Trudy. Poor Don. How ironic that if he did hurt Joan, he lost Trudy in much the same way. An injury left too long untended.

I glanced back at Don just as he straightened. Our eyes met, and I was rocked back on my heels by the emotion I saw there.

Anger. Fierce, white-hot anger.

FIFTEEN

Trying to swallow the lump in my throat, I slipped into Patrick Marten's viewing/funeral and took my place at the end of the condolence line slowly moving toward Liz Marten.

Pat's death is not your fault, I told myself.

Of course it's not, I answered. *I know that.*

Then why do you feel so guilty?

It was my car.

And you think that makes it your fault?

I just want to make them hurt less.

It was a good thing Jack couldn't hear me talking to myself.

"It's your fix-it complex," he'd say in that mocking tone he always used whenever I told him how I hurt for people and wanted them to be okay. "It's your God complex. Why do you think you're the one who should deal with every crisis? Why do you think you're the one who should make everything better? Just a bit presumptuous, don't you think? You're Merry Kramer, girl reporter, not Mother Teresa."

Suddenly, standing in line waiting to talk to Liz

Marten, I experienced the strong mental zap of profound insight. I felt like a cartoon character with a lightbulb suddenly going off over my head. I had to force myself not to look around to see if others noticed me glowing in an electric halo.

It wasn't presumptuous to try and help! God made me with the desire to help, and He seemed to give me the ability to comfort people. It was a God-thing, not a me-thing! It was good, and Jack was wrong.

"Merry!" Annie had to say my name several times, I was so lost in thought. She gave me a great hug. "Mom will be so glad you came."

"Are you sure? I feel like I come equipped with bad associations."

Annie shook her head. "Truth to tell, Mom thinks you're pretty nice. And she loved your article on Pat today. It was kind and accurate."

Liz turned from comforting the man and woman ahead of me. "Merry." She hugged me.

All I wanted to do was cry, and I blinked like mad to keep from weeping. I wasn't successful. "I'm so sorry, Liz," I blubbered.

She smiled crookedly. "Aren't we all. But what about you? Are you all right? I read about Andy shooting at you."

"I'm fine," I said.

She looked skeptical. "I'd feel terrible forever if anything happened to you because of us."

Guilt. The one emotion there's always plenty of.

Hannah stood beside Liz, her hair washed and curled today, but the life still gone from her face. Liz reached to the girl and slid an arm around her waist.

"You remember Merry, don't you, Hannah?" Liz asked.

Hannah shuddered at Liz's touch, and Liz drew her closer still.

"It's not your fault, sweetheart," she said, obviously not for the first time. "It's not your fault."

Hannah smiled wanly. Words, even the warm words of Pat's mother, couldn't make the guilty feelings stop.

I hugged Hannah. "She's right, you know," I said. "I feel guilty, too, because it was my car, but I know I'm not. And neither are you. You aren't responsible for Andy."

Hannah looked at me. "I know that in my head, but I can't believe it in my heart." She turned and walked over to stand beside Pat's casket.

Liz watched the girl. "I hope her trust in God is deep enough to handle this. Believe me, that's the only way to live with the pain."

I had used untold tissues by the time the service was over, but I left more comforted than I had felt at Trudy's. When the congregation sang "It Is Well With My Soul," I knew that here in this little church, in spite of the questions and the pain, God was allowed to be God.

I didn't go to the cemetery. I had an article to write, and another trip to another cemetery on this gray and dismal day would make the writing impossible. I'd be too spent.

Not surprisingly, I found Don hard at work at his neat desk before the great window. I knew he'd have to do something to work off the emotional complexities of his loss of Trudy, and what suited him better than getting lost in his beloved paper? A workaholic like him certainly wasn't going to go calmly to Stanton McGilpin's for the after-funeral meal. Not for him the chatter and comfort of people who shared his grief. Not with his secret pain and that anger gnawing at him.

I watched him staring at his terminal. I knew why he hurt, but I hadn't the vaguest idea why he hated, or whom.

I blinked. Hated? Don hated? Where had that come from? I had no idea, but I *knew* I was right.

Don hated.

Poor Don.

As I chewed on that thought, I turned on my terminal and typed my password. *Whiskers.* Not very secret if you'd ever been to my house, but I'd never invited anyone from the paper to my house. Besides, who wanted my work? We're not talking supersecret documents here. We're talking reporting on community events open to anyone who cared to go to them. We're talking adequate writing, not the stuff of Pulitzer prizes.

Two special people were laid to rest today in Amhearst, two people who died violently and before their time.

I wrote about the funerals for a bit, comparing and contrasting them. I mentioned the love obvious at both and the sorrow of the bereaved. I mentioned the endearing simplicity of Pat's and the affectionate pomp of Trudy's. And I got more and more melancholy.

I save my text and went to my e-mail. Maybe there'd be a message from Sam to cheer me up. He wrote me regularly from school, and I loved hearing from him. It was great to read his few lines and to respond with a few of my own.

Merry, what in the world are you doing? I talked to Mom last night, and she's certain you'll be murdered in your bed. If you are, she'll blame herself forever for letting you leave Pittsburgh. I recommend you do your utmost to stay alive. It'd probably be best for both of you.

I grinned. He was such a sweet guy.

Sam, not to worry. I plan to stay alive as long as I possibly can—which I think will be until I'm about ninety. They won't let me go anywhere alone, anyway. Oh, they did let me go to a couple of funerals today without an escort, but they're keeping a good eye on me. Thanks for caring, though. Just don't let worrying about me get in the way of your schoolwork. Gag! I sound just like Mom!

I clicked Send, then hit the icon for my next message. Up it flashed, and I began to read.

I didn't do it! I mean it! I didn't shoot at you! I didn't ever do anything to you. I mean, why should I? You don't know anything about what happened to Pat. That's what I was trying to tell you last night.

I stared at my screen in disbelief. My heart was racing and my stomach had that funny I-might-throw-up feeling. I checked the sender's name immediately, though I knew who it was. *Witz*. As in *Gershowitz*.

I didn't do it! I mean it!

He's good, I thought. *He knows how to get to me. I know he's a killer and a liar, and yet I want to know why he claims he's innocent. I want to understand him and his story.* I read on:

But I do know something you'd like to know. You're a reporter, right? So you want a great story, right? Well, I got one for you. You won't believe it.

He was right. I didn't believe it. Andy Gershowitz was e-mailing me!

The paper printed its e-mail address, Amhearst-News.com, for letters to the editor. Working from that address, he'd probably sent the same message to every permutation of Merrileigh Kramer he could think of. And MKramer wouldn't have taken much imagination.

Meet me, OK? We need to talk face-to-face. Meet me at Brandywine Steel at 5:45. I won't hurt you. I promise. But I got to tell someone what I saw before the cops get me. I want to tell you. And believe me, you want to hear.

He was right. I did want to hear. Every reporter wants to hear when the object of a manhunt wants to talk.

I'll be waiting by the door on the east side. It's sort of dark there, but don't be afraid. I'll protect you.

The irony of that last line made me smile. I could just hear Curt's response or Sergeant Poole's.

I've only got one rule, and that's that you've got to come alone. I don't want any big guys with glasses chasing me all over town again. Understand? And don't tell your boss, either. I mean it. If I see anybody with you, I'm leaving before you even see me.

I could understand his feelings after last night's chase. He needn't worry. I'd come alone.

If you don't show, I'll try again tomorrow.

I was struck by the need he felt for contact with a person who would listen. Who better than a woman with a fix-it complex, a woman called by God to listen to the problems of anyone who'd talk?

I hit Reply and typed I'll see you at 5:45.

After I sent my answer, I reread the original message again and again. The way he worded his comments sounded like he wanted to talk about something other than his own experiences. Maybe I could talk him into surrendering! Now *there* would be a story.

My stomach still felt funny, but now it was the flutter of anticipation. The adrenaline was flowing big-time.

I glanced at the clock. Four-thirty. An hour and fifteen minutes to wait.

"Merry, what are you doing?" Don's voice cracked like a whip.

I froze, doubtless looking guilty as sin. Don was

watching me from across the room, and he looked decidedly unfriendly. When all this death stuff had calmed down, I'd have to ask him what I had done to make him so angry. I couldn't stand having my boss displeased with me all the time.

I had a terrible thought. Was I the one he was thinking of when he looked up from Trudy's casket at the cemetery? Was the anger there because he saw me? Was I the one he hated?

I quickly dismissed that thought. You have to have a reason to hate someone. He and I never had enough contact to generate the emotions necessary for hate. He might be unhappy with me as an employee. But hate? No, not hate.

"I'm not doing anything special," I said, smiling in what I hoped was a friendly fashion. I could feel my face flush, and I knew I looked false and suspicious.

Don got up from his desk and started toward me, his frown firmly in place.

I glanced from him to my monitor. And don't tell your boss, either. I mean it.

I couldn't let Don see this letter. He'd want to come with me, or worse still, go in my place. Or he'd strong-arm me into calling the cops.

I hit the Close File icon and sent Andy's letter from the screen. Then I hit another icon and another until I was at the main menu by the time Don reached my desk. He looked at my screen, then at me.

I'm so lousy at looking innocent when I'm not.

SIXTEEN

Don and I stared at my inoffensive screen. I assumed that he had seen my hands flashing madly about and knew I had closed out something I didn't want him to see. But he said nothing about it. Neither did I.

"How's the funeral article coming?" he finally asked. The tone of voice was genial enough, but when he looked at me, his eyes were hard.

"Pretty well," I said, hitting the right commands and calling it up. "I've been working hard on it." Which was certainly true.

He leaned over my shoulder, hand resting on my desk, and read for a minute. He nodded. "Just so I have the completed piece on my desk by Monday at nine."

"Don't worry. You will." I hit the Save button. "Well, I think I'll leave now," I said. "Enough work for a weekend."

Don smiled thinly. He was still leaning over me, still resting his hand on my desk, and I was uncomfortably aware of his somehow threatening bulk. Threatening? He was the same man I had run to in my parking lot three nights ago. How had he become threatening?

"Spending the evening with Curt?" There was definitely malice in his voice now.

I looked at him sharply though I kept my voice mild. "Something wrong with that?"

He shrugged but said nothing.

"Why do you dislike Curt so?" I asked.

"Because he dislikes me," Don said, and I saw the malevolence I'd seen at the cemetery.

Was it Curt he hated? Was his aversion to me because of his abhorrence of Curt?

"Everyone thinks Curt is this wonderful Christian," Don said suddenly, spite falling like drool from his lips. "If they only knew his nasty, vindictive side, they'd feel differently." His eyes bored into mine, and I was a butterfly pinned to a board. "Don't say I didn't warn you," he muttered. "Though why I bother, I don't know. You deserve each other." He spun crisply on his heel and walked away.

Stung, I stared at his retreating back. What was this *you deserve each other* bit? Where had that come from?

I could understand why he might not like Curt, especially if he was aware that Curt thought he had killed Joan. I had to assume that he knew about Curt's suspicions.

But what had I ever done to make him dislike me? Again I thought back over the three months I'd been at *The News*. Don and I had done very well together until these past few days. Even the night I found Pat's body in my trunk, Don had been friendly, supportive, even mildly affectionate in a distant sort of way.

Aside from the attempts on my life, the only thing different about the past three days was that I had met Curt.

It always came back to Curt. Which meant it always came back to Joan.

Don collapsed angrily into his chair, his face stormy and tight. I wondered whether his little temper tantrum had given me a small glimpse of what Joan had come to see. Did she frequently wonder, like me, what she had done to provoke him?

I got up, collected my purse and gloves, and slipped on my coat.

Don't say I didn't warn you. You deserve each other.

It would take more than my coat to ease the chill of Don's words.

When I stepped outside, it was into a world made mysterious by fog so thick that I wondered how there was enough breathable oxygen in the atmosphere to sustain human life. I stared through the gray curtain, listening to my spiky hair droop. Wednesday night sleet. Friday snow. Saturday warmer temperatures and fog rising from the melting snow.

Hooray for Pennsylvania winters.

I climbed into my rental car and drove across the street to the parking area behind City Hall. After all Curt had done for me, I felt I had to tell him that I had an appointment. I didn't want him to worry needlessly.

I also didn't want him to tell me I shouldn't meet Andy—which I had no doubt he'd do. I wasn't going to let him get in the way of this story any more than I had let Don. I was going to meet Andy regardless of what anyone thought or said. I was a reporter, and this was my story!

But what was I going to say that would keep Curt from having a fit?

As it turned out, it was a nonproblem. I found the Brennan Room almost empty, though the pictures looked as good today as they had last night. Curt was across the room with his back to me, talking with a man in a pair of jeans and a plaid flannel shirt. I walked toward them. They were standing in front of a huge painting, easily five feet by six. The placard with its $6000 price tag was one of the few without a red dot on it.

As I got near the men, it became obvious that they were dickering about the price of the picture.

"Six thousand is a bit steep," the man in the jeans said. He looked like six bucks would be a bit steep.

"Well, Mr. Harrison, four thousand dollars is a bit low for the time and planning that went into this painting," Curt answered.

Mr. Harrison as in Mr. Harrison, the president of the Amhearst Central Bank, one of the few independent, community banks remaining in our area? Mr. Harrison was facing me and I looked at him more closely. The jeans might be well-worn and the plaid shirt frayed, but the eyes were alert and eager in the business of buying and selling.

I certainly wasn't going to interrupt what might turn out to be one of Curt's more important sales. I made like I had come over to study the painting itself.

A Chester County fieldstone house sat beside a pond rimmed with cattails and evergreens. A spring-house sat at the edge of the pond, where a stream lined with tall grasses flowed frothing over some rocks. The evening sky was streaked with the peaches and golds of a shimmering sunset, and a flock of Canada geese were descending to the waiting pond.

"What do you want to do with this painting?" I heard Curt ask.

"Hang it in the bank. Think I've got a house big enough to handle something that size? Evil rumors, Curt. Just because I built with a view doesn't mean I built big. How about forty-five hundred?"

I turned away as Curt said, "How about six thousand?"

Mr. Harrison laughed, obviously having a wonderful time.

I looked around for someone I could leave my message with. There was no one else in the Brennan Room but the three of us. I wandered down a hallway past closed and locked doors, looking for a caretaker or something. A weekend silence gripped the place.

I gave up and decided I'd have to leave a note. I pulled my small notebook from my purse and wrote:

Curt, I have a business meeting at 5:45. I'll be back by 7:00. Don't worry. I'll be fine. Merry

I looked around the Brennan Room. Where could I put this paper so that Curt would find it? If I laid it on the table that had held food last night and held nothing today, it'd be too easy to miss. I certainly couldn't attach it to a painting.

The front door. I should tape it to the front door. He'd see it there. The only trouble was that I had no tape.

I looked around and spotted some name tags on the edge of the table. I grabbed a name tag, tore off one end and used it to stick the note to the front glass.

Feeling virtuous and altogether a most considerate person, I drove home to change my clothes.

I hung my mist-dampened black gabardine pantsuit

on the closet door to dry, folded the black, gray and rose scarf and tossed the white silk turtleneck in the hamper. I pulled on black jeans and a red turtleneck. Then I dug out my favorite red-and-black checkerboard sweater. I always felt chipper when I wore it, and I needed to feel fine and feisty this evening, because my stomach was feeling queasy again.

I looked at Whiskers, who sat on the bed and watched me through sleepy eyes.

"I wonder," I asked him as I brushed my sticky, sagging hair, "how many newspaper people get ulcers."

He shook his head and reached a back paw up to scratch lazily at his ear. He made a satisfied groaning noise deep in his throat.

I grabbed him and gave him a hug. "You'll never suffer from ulcers, bub. Can someone die of lethargy? If so, watch out. You've been lethally stricken."

I put him down on the bed, and he immediately closed his eyes. I patted his head and decided he was a pretty good family substitute, especially considering the problems in the families I had dealt with recently.

There were the Martens with their love and loss and faith, the McGilpins with their lives ripped apart and the Carlyles, all gone but Curt.

For the first time I was struck by the idea of the Gershowitz family. They were also being ripped apart, just like the others.

Who were the Gershowitzes? What were the parents like? Were there brothers and sisters? How did this week's events affect them all? Were they worried about Andy? Ashamed of him?

Did they feel guilty like Hannah?

I had seen a photo of Lucinda Gershowitz, Andy's mom, taken at the Fall Fete to benefit Amhearst Community Hospital, and knew she served with Don on the hospital's Board of Directors. In the news photo she looked sleek and soigné in her formal gown. I tried to recall Mr. Gershowitz, assuming he'd been pictured with her, but all I conjured up was fuzz.

I sat slowly on the edge of the bed and wondered what it was like to have a son who had killed someone and attempted to kill someone else.

My parents were so proud of Sam. What if he weren't such a great guy? What if he were actually a nasty guy? What if he killed someone? I shook my head. I couldn't begin to imagine what it must be like.

I went to the kitchen and rooted in the drawer for the phone book. Looking under Gershowitz, I found three listed, but only one had an Amhearst exchange. I punched in the number. While I waited for an answer, I glanced at the clock. Five-fifteen. Plenty of time.

The phone was answered on the first ring.

"Hello?" a woman's breathless voice said.

"Mrs. Gershowitz?"

"Yes?" she said, at once hesitant and disappointed. Not only was she uncertain about who I was; she was disappointed I wasn't someone else.

"My name's Merrileigh Kramer, from *The News*."

A hissing noise came down the line. "What do *you* want? Haven't you done enough, writing about my Andy like that?"

"Mrs. Gershowitz, I haven't ever written about

Andy. Other reporters have been handling the information that the police provide. I've written about Patrick Marten and about the attempts on my life."

"And you think it was Andy. I know it! And it wasn't! He's a good boy, my Andy is."

I was struck by the raw desperation in her voice. This wasn't the sophisticated woman in the ball gown. This was a hurting mother trying to protect her cub.

"I'm certain all this has been very hard on you," I said for want of anything better. I wasn't going to debate Andy's guilt or innocence with her, the one person who had the most to lose in the whole issue—except for Andy, of course.

"Hard on me?" Her answer was a sob.

I told myself I couldn't feel sorry for her and asked, "Have you had any contact with Andy since Wednesday?"

"Of course not," she said, and the lie traveled as smoothly through the air as the truth would have.

"Were you expecting to hear from him when you answered the phone just now?"

"Of course not." Another lie.

"Where do you think he is?"

"How would I know?"

But she does know, I thought. *The woman is not good at dissembling. I hope Andy's not depending on her to help him get away. She'll give whatever plans they have away whether she means to or not. She's too desperate on his behalf.*

"If you could talk to him," I asked, "what would you say?"

"I'd tell him I loved him."

I waited, but that was all she said. "You wouldn't tell him to turn himself in?"

"And go to jail?" Her voice went up at the end at the horror of the thought. And it was horrible. "Never!"

I was surprised. "Don't you think it's dangerous for him to be hiding from the police? What if they find him and he gets shot or something?"

"They won't find him."

Was that wishful thinking or the words of a rich woman used to getting her own way? "Why do you say that?"

She'd obviously decided she'd said too much. "It's harassment is what it is. Harassment pure and simple." Some of the imperiousness that I could picture going with the ball gown edged her voice. "They just decided to pick on Andy. That's what it is. He's a good boy, but do they believe me when I say that? Oh, no, not them." Steel and spite filled the words. "It's a vendetta against my son!"

"But, Mrs. Gershowitz, what about his fingerprints on the murder weapon?"

Such evidence was not a problem to Andy's mother. "He was set up. He was!"

"Someone told me that Andy had a pretty bad temper," I said.

"Lies," said his mother. "He—"

Through the phone, I heard someone shout, "Lucinda! Who are you taking to?"

Lucinda Gershowitz's hand clamped imperfectly over the mouthpiece. "It's a private conversation, Harold."

A man's gruff voice repeated, "Who are you talking to?"

I could picture the two of them staring at each other. Would she tell him who she was talking to? Whose will was the stronger, hers or his?

She capitulated. "It's that Merrileigh Kramer of *The News*."

There was a moment of silence while I waited to see what would happen. I heard fumbling noises, and Mr. Gershowitz suddenly spit at me, "You write a message in your paper to that kid who *used* to be mine, lady."

"Harold!" The pain in his wife's voice was terrible to hear.

"Tell him," Harold Gershowitz continued, "he'll get no help from me. No sympathy. No money. Definitely no money. And he'd better not look for anything from his mother, either, because I won't let her get involved. And that's final!"

I heard Mrs. Gershowitz shout, "You can't stop me! It's my money! And don't you raise your hand to me, Harold Gershowitz. You think I won't tell the police? They're here all the time, anyway, looking for our boy. *Our* boy!" she repeated and began to sob. Her wailing grew louder, closer to the phone. I could picture Mr. Gershowitz relenting, reaching out and pulling his wife to him, the forgotten telephone probably now held behind her back.

"Our boy." He repeated his wife's words but without the heat of his previous comments. There was a moment's silence. "No," he finally said slowly and softly. "He's your boy now, Lucy. Not mine." I heard his pain and hurt along with his unyielding repudiation. "He's shamed me through and through. How can

I ever hold my head up again in this town? How can I ever make a living again? How can I ever expect to have a decent life? No matter where I go, no matter what I do, someone will always know. 'Oh, yeah, there goes the murderer's father.'"

He sobbed a little himself, then cleared his throat. His voice became hard again. "How could he have done this?"

And he hung up.

SEVENTEEN

I pulled into the parking lot at 5:47 p.m. according to the clock on the dash. My headlights bounced back at me in the fog, and I turned them off. I climbed out and stood leaning against the car. It took my eyes a couple of minutes to adjust to the different shades of gray swirling in the weak light of a streetlamp.

I wasn't certain my heart and nerves would ever return to normal.

Not that I was exactly afraid. For some reason Andy didn't frighten me—which might say more about my mental prowess than anything. But I was edgy and uncertain. If I knew anything about Andy, it was that he was volatile.

I reached into the pocket of my red barn coat and felt the little voice-activated tape recorder I had shoved there. I pressed the On button and softly stated the time and place. There'd be no misquotes from me tonight.

A large gray building reared out of the fog in front of me, stretching into the mists and disappearing. A pair of signs at the edge of the parking area provided the only splashes of color, one sign black and reading Brandywine Steel in white letters edged with crimson.

A smaller white sign announced in similar letters that visitors were to follow the arrow west.

I began walking toward the east side of the building, just as Andy had told me.

My shoulder blades twitched, and I looked quickly behind me, not really expecting anyone to be there but incapable of resisting the compulsion. All I saw was the gray and misty ocean in which I was immersed. I thought sardonically that I had become one of those imbecilic gothic heroines, right down to the fog.

I hurried on, my muted footsteps swallowed in the *ka-thump, ka-thump* of my heart in my ears.

Suddenly a doorway, utilitarian and the same gray as the building, became visible. I stared at it, uncertain. Somehow knocking seemed foolish.

Knock, knock.

Who's there?

Andy.

Andy who?

Andy walks with me and he talks with me.

"Andy?" I whispered.

"You came!" His voice, heavy with relief, came eerily out of the thick night air.

"You asked me to." I stared as hard as I could through the grayness, but I couldn't see him. Still, the voice was right, the one I'd heard last night by the lilac tree.

"Pull your car up under the overhang so the cops won't see it," he instructed. "They keep driving by all the time. And leave your purse and cell phone in the car."

I did as he asked and the car was swallowed in the fog and shadows. I felt somewhat naked without my cell. Not that I expected to need help. Not really.

I walked to the door again, and he said, "Come on in."

I'd assumed he was just standing in the shadows, ready to reveal himself dramatically when he chose. For the first time I realized he was inside the building.

I slid through the door he held open, and immediately the acrid odor of cordite and grease hit me.

"How did you get in here without setting off the alarms?" I asked.

"I work here," he said.

"Sure, I know that. But not everyone who works here has access to the security codes or keys or whatever you use."

"Yeah," he said, "but not everybody's family owns the place."

"Your father owns Brandywine Steel?"

"My mom," he said. "Her father started the company, and Dad married the boss's daughter when he was a welder like me. Made Grandpop furious because he wanted Mom to marry better than a high-school dropout." I could sense rather than see Andy shrug his shoulders. "He got used to it in time. Now Dad runs the place, but Mom still controls the money. I guess Grandpop never completely forgave Dad."

So Dad, who felt Andy had shamed and ruined him, had risen above his origins. And Mom, the boss's daughter who had believed in a welder once, now believed her other welder was a good boy in spite of the hard evidence. And she still controlled the purse for both of them.

Now the phone conversation I'd had with the Gershowitzes made more sense. My only questions were how did Mrs. Gershowitz plan to get her money to

Andy and how did she think she'd get away with it without being detected? And what did he plan to do with the money? Where did he plan to go?

Andy started walking across a cavernous space, a small flashlight pointed at his feet. Several night-lights shone at intervals from the steel struts that held up the roof high above, but they shed little light. I decided their job was to create shadows, and they fulfilled their purpose quite well.

I followed Andy closely, uncomfortable in the vast, echoing expanse. If my lilac tree could hide a gang of bad guys, this place could house a whole army.

"It's spooky in here," I muttered as a great piece of machinery loomed up beside us.

"That's just a large lathe," Andy said, becoming my tour guide. "And that's a roll bedding machine and that's a portable welding unit. Those—" he indicated a pair of cylinders that looked like miniature rockets "—are the gas tanks for the welding. And over there's the overhead crane and that's a grinding unit."

I made impressed noises, not telling him that to my unsophisticated eye all his undoubtedly wonderful and highly technical equipment looked like black blobs with scary shadows. I just stayed close to his light so I wouldn't trip over the cables that snaked across the floor like silent reptiles slithering from shadow pool to shadow pool.

Suddenly he jogged slightly to the right. "Watch it," he said, the penlight shining on a wooden pallet about a foot off the floor. On it were three slabs of steel waiting to be made into something useful. I carefully stepped around it.

"That shouldn't be there," Andy said, disapproval sharp in his voice. "It's sticking out into the safe area."

"The safe area?"

"See those lines?" He pointed his penlight at worn yellow lines that went down each side of the area where we were. "They mark the walkways where it's always supposed to be safe to walk. OSHA requires them. Whoever left that pallet there is in violation."

I made an understanding noise.

"We don't take safety lightly around here," he said. "If the shop were operating, you'd have to wear safety glasses and a hard hat. You can't be too careful with dangerous equipment like we've got."

I listened to his little lecture on safety and wondered how he had learned these secondary truths so well and missed the primary ones about human relationships. Don't let a pallet stick out over the yellow lines, but go ahead and bash in the head of an innocent guy who gets in your way.

I decided, wisely for once, that this was not a good observation with which to begin our conversation.

"You liked working here, didn't you?" I asked instead.

He nodded. "I do. Someday it'll all be mine."

Oh, boy, I thought, catching the difference in the verb tenses he and I had used. He certainly wasn't letting reality interfere with his plans for the future.

The safe area became a sort of aisle between dividers that looked ragged and insubstantial even as they flashed Andy's penlight back at me. I reached out and touched large sheets of some kind of polyvinyl tied to tall metal poles balanced in old tires.

Suddenly Andy cut left between two of the dividers.

I followed him around the corner and found myself in a good-size cubicle, not a neat, clean one like in an office, but a work space formed by the polyvinyl sheets and littered with tools and equipment lying in organized disarray. At one end of the worktable sat a laptop, open and operating, its electronic gray light adding to the eeriness of this place.

"This is my welding area," Andy said, unmistakable pride in his voice. "Those are called welding shields." He pointed to the dividers. "They block the arcs of light when we're welding. Some of the sheets are yellow or light blue, and they block the light okay. Some are black, and they do a real good job. I have black ones around my area."

Nothing but the best for the heir apparent.

"Each of the welders has his own area?" I asked.

Andy nodded and flashed his light to show me his work space. I saw his welder's mask and an acetylene torch lying on the large worktable. Other tools I couldn't identify lay here and there. A large, stationary fan rose like a basketball backboard on a long pole in one corner.

"So tell me," I said, deciding it was time to get down to business. I had more than enough information to set the scene for my readers. "Why did you ask me to meet you here tonight? What do you want from me?"

"No, you got it wrong. I don't want anything *from* you. It's what I'm going to give *to* you. But first I gotta know something." He hesitated. "Do you pay sources? I know the cops pay for information. I see it all the time on TV. I thought maybe you could pay me, too."

I thought of the ten dollars in my jeans pocket. Somehow I didn't think that was the amount he had in mind.

"It'll be worth it, believe me," he assured me.

"Oh, I believe it will be, but we don't pay for stories, Andy. I think the cops sometimes use confiscated drug money for expenses like that." Talk about getting your information from TV. "But we don't have drug money lying around the office. And if money for informants is in our budget, no one's told me."

He swore and let out a great sigh.

Suddenly I got worried. "You're still going to tell me whatever it is, aren't you?"

He nodded. "Yeah, 'cause I've got to get the cops off my back. It was worth a try for the extra money. I like extra money. Especially now."

"Why?" I asked, trying to sound all innocent and eager.

"Wouldn't you like to know," he said, and his voice suddenly dripped anger.

"I would like to know," I said, not backing down. "It'd be a great part of the story."

"Well, it's not a part you're getting." And I could tell by the tone of finality that I wasn't.

"So what do you want to tell me?" I asked.

He looked at me across the dark shadows of his cubicle. "Remember when you were driving home Wednesday night on Oak Lane and you almost hit someone?"

I looked at him sharply. "Of course I remember. It scared me to death. But how do you know about it?"

"I was the guy you almost hit."

"What?"

"Yeah," he said, and I could hear the smile in his voice. He liked surprising me. "That was me."

I recalled the image of the man standing ready to cross the street and felt a flash of the terror I'd experienced when my car had slid uncontrollably toward him. I waited for a spasm of recognition, one of those *aha!* moments like I'd had in line at Pat's funeral, but none occurred. The blurry image of memory remained just that. If he hadn't told me he was the one, I'd never have known.

"What were you doing out there in the sleet and rain?" I asked. "Do you live around there?"

"No. We live outside town on a gentleman's farm. At least that's what Dad likes to call it. Our house is big, bigger than Grandpop's."

Obviously beating Grandpop was important. I suspected beating everybody was important. "So you still live at home?"

"Sure do," he agreed easily. "I'm not crazy. I know a good deal when I see one. And when Hannah and I get married, I'll build a house for us on the farm."

I decided not to touch that piece of denial with a ten-foot pole.

"Do you have brothers and sisters?" I asked instead.

He shook his head. "Only child." He grinned. "More money for me."

I looked in wonder at this man/child, this mass of contradictions and wishful thinking, and returned to our topic for the evening. "So why were you near Trudy McGilpin's?"

"I was going to go see her."

He's surprised me again. "To see her? At that time of night?"

"I knew I needed a good lawyer, and she was the only one I knew about."

I rubbed my forehead. "You knew you needed a good lawyer because you'd killed Pat Marten?"

"Yeah." I barely heard the word. "I still can't believe it, you know? We were talking, him and me, just talking about Hannah. And suddenly there he was, lying on the garage floor, his head all bloody."

I sighed. It was all so very sad,

Andy looked sharply at me. "You aren't going to write any more about Pat, are you? He's gotten enough glory already, and that isn't what I want to talk about. Besides, I'll deny the whole conversation."

My hand found the tape recorder and checked the On button. It was properly depressed. He could deny all he wanted. "The police already know all about what happened, Andy. You know that. They have the wrench."

He set his penlight down on his workbench and picked up a wrench of his own. "The big thing was just lying there on his workbench with all this other stuff." His voice grew whiny. "Why'd he have to put it where I'd grab it? Why couldn't he have put a screwdriver or a pair of pliers there? Then I'd just have a guy who was mad at me for popping him one instead of a dead guy."

He sounded genuinely miffed at Pat.

"What did he say that upset you so?"

"Well, I told him he had to leave Hannah alone. She was my girl, and he actually thought he was going to marry her!" As he talked, the whine left and the volume rose. "Can you believe that? My Hannah!

Everybody knows she's mine. She's been mine since ninth grade. She belongs to me!"

"Maybe she didn't want to belong to you anymore?" I suggested softly and unwisely.

He turned on me and grabbed my arm, frightening me for the first time.

"Don't you start with me too, lady!" he hissed. "Remember, that's what Patsy said, and you know what happened to him." He glared at me to be sure I understood what he was saying.

I understood all right. My mouth was dry, and I worried that my knees were about to go on strike. But I wasn't a member of Brenda Starr's sisterhood for nothing!

I cleared my throat and asked, "What exactly did Pat say to you?"

"'Maybe she doesn't want to belong to you anymore,' is what he said. She doesn't want to belong to me? Of course she does! Why wouldn't she?"

He stared at me fiercely, and I thought for one awful moment that he actually wanted an answer. I was searching for something to say that wouldn't make him madder when he continued.

"He shouldn't have said that! It was his fault, what happened! His fault! 'Andy, it's her choice, not yours,' he said. Like she'd choose Patsy over me!"

"Easy, Andy." I struggled to make my voice soft and nonthreatening.

"Easy, Andy," he mocked.

I put my hand gently over his where it painfully squeezed my forearm, trying not to look at the wrench clutched in his other fist. "Andy, you're hurting me."

He glared at me through slitted eyes, then pushed me away, spinning me off balance for a minute as he turned abruptly to his welding table. He swept his arm, the wrench still clutched in his fist, across the surface, sending the mask, the torch and other tools spinning like pieces of shrapnel. I noticed, though, that he took care not to damage his laptop.

As the crashing noises echoed around us, I thought I heard another clatter beyond the welding shield. I glanced at Andy, but he'd obviously heard nothing besides the din he'd created.

He stood with his back against his table, and his voice shook as he said triumphantly, "Well, he didn't get her, did he?"

EIGHTEEN

"No, he didn't get her," I repeated softly. "You're absolutely right."

We stood, silent for a minute. I had no idea what Andy was thinking, but a great pall of depression wrapped itself about me.

"Did it ever occur to you that if you love someone, you want to make them happy?" I asked.

"What?" He looked genuinely confused.

"If you love someone, you want them to be happy."

He stared at me, waiting for more. "So what's your point?" he finally asked.

"Maybe you could have made Hannah happy by letting her marry Pat."

He laughed, a short, staccato burst. "That's funny. Hannah happy with Pat? That's really funny."

"Do you think she's happy now?"

He shrugged. "I don't know why not. Now she can come with me when I leave."

"Is that why you're still in town? You're waiting for Hannah to agree to come with you?"

He nodded. "That's one reason."

"And the other's your mother's money? You're waiting to get it?"

"Can't get it until Monday," he kindly explained. "The banks are closed."

Well, that answered one of the questions that had been plaguing me.

"Have you talked to Hannah?" I asked. "Have you tried to contact her?"

He looked grim. "She didn't want to talk to me, even when I told her I did it for her. I mean, I didn't really. It was an accident. But I wanted to impress her, I guess."

Poor Hannah! No wonder she looked and acted so guilt-plagued. My heart ached for her.

"She hung up on me," he said unhappily, "but she'll come around now that Pat's not here to bother her anymore."

I pressed my lips together and actually put my hand over my mouth to restrain all the comments about his stupidity and selfishness that I wanted to scream at him. When I finally felt I could trust myself again, I said grimly, "But Pat and Hannah aren't what you wanted to talk to me about."

"You're absolutely right." He smiled winsomely. "I haven't given you your story yet."

He lay the wrench on the worktable, and I must admit I breathed more easily as a result.

"But I got a question for you first," he said, turning to me.

"Another one?" I tried to look calm, but I was feeling so tense that I could hardly stay still. I'm a fidgeter under the best of circumstances—which this certainly wasn't.

"Why'd you come here tonight?" he asked.

"You asked me."

"Yeah, but lots of people still wouldn't have come. Or they'd have called the cops or something."

"What would you have done if I had called the cops?"

"Oh, there's plenty of places around here where they'd never find me." His eyes flew to a bank of cabinets against the wall.

"Is this—" I indicated the building "—where you've been the past three days?"

He grinned. "Wouldn't you like to know?"

I nodded and forced myself to smile back. "It'd be great for my story."

He shrugged. "Maybe I'll show you my spot. Then again maybe I won't."

Cute, I thought. *So cute.*

"So why'd you come?" he repeated. "Aren't you scared of me?"

I shook my head. "Maybe I should be, but I'm not. And you seemed to need to talk to me. I decided to take the risk."

"Who knows you're here?"

I took a deep breath and told him the truth. "No one."

"So I could whap you on the head, too, and no one would know?"

"Not until Monday morning when the guys came in to work and found me, I guess. Of course, if you did me in, I couldn't write about your evening at the mayor's."

We looked at each other, a strange sort of understanding between us.

"Like I was saying," Andy said as he hoisted himself onto his worktable. He began kicking his legs back and forth, back and forth. "I was standing there trying to get up the nerve to ring the mayor's doorbell."

"Did you hesitate because you knew she was sick?"

He shook his head. "I didn't know that. Was she really sick?"

"She must have been. She'd canceled some meetings. And we know she passed out and hit her head."

"Oh, yeah." He grinned like I had said something funny. "She passed out and hit her head."

I waited, but he didn't share the joke. Instead he continued his story.

"I was sort of scared to go to her door because I'd never met her. I saw her picture in the paper a lot, but I never talked with her or anything. I mean, would she be snotty or would she be nice?"

"What did you want her to do for you?"

"Be my lawyer," he said, stating the obvious.

"I know that," I said. "But what did you think that meant?"

"Well, she'd help me out. She'd listen to me and tell me what to do and help me hide."

"Help you hide?" I was startled.

He nodded. "Yeah."

"But lawyers don't hide people from the police," I said.

"Sure they do. Like in *The Client*."

"But that was just a book. A novel."

"It was?" He seemed surprised. "I saw the movie on TV a couple of times. The lawyer hid this kid from the cops."

"But that kid was innocent of any crime. Certainly he didn't kill anyone."

"Yeah, but she hid him. And she got him a new life. He flew off in a plane at the end, and the FBI let him go. That's what I wanted the mayor to do for me."

"But that was because that kid was innocent," I repeated. "And besides, it was only a novel and a movie based on a novel."

"Well, they couldn't have made it into a book or a movie if it wasn't true."

"Sure they could have. That's what a novel is," I said. "A made-up story."

He shook his head. "She would have done it. Just like Reggie Love in the movie. I know."

"I don't think so, Andy."

"Why not?" he asked belligerently.

"Because you're not innocent. You killed Pat. Everybody knows it."

"But I didn't mean to."

I nodded. "So they'll call it involuntary manslaughter instead of murder, and the penalty won't be as serious. But you're still guilty."

It was obvious that Andy didn't like that idea at all.

"Have you thought about turning yourself in?" I asked.

"So they can send me to jail? Are you kidding? I'm not going to jail!"

"But you can't run forever," I said. "You're bound to get caught, and by running you're just making things worse for yourself."

"Nothing's worse than jail. I've seen the jail movies, too. Besides, I'm not hanging around here much longer."

"Where are you going?" I asked.

"Do you think I'm dumb enough to tell you? You'll just put it in the papers."

I grinned wryly. "You've got my number," I said. "So tell me more about that rainy night."

"Well, it was just before you came along and almost ran me over." He glared, making sure I realized that I should feel bad for scaring him like that. "This guy comes running out of the mayor's house. I mean, he was mad!"

"A guy came out of the mayor's house? Are you sure it was her house?"

He nodded. "I looked up the address before I went over. And there's the sign."

"What sign?"

"There's this little sign hanging on her light post that says McGilpin. I know because I checked."

"Before or after the man came out? Before or after I almost hit you?"

"Uh, I went back the next day," he said quickly, too quickly. "After I heard she was dead, you know? I wanted to be sure the guy really came from her house."

"And he did?"

"And he did."

"And he was mad?"

"He was burning up. I could practically see the steam from across the street. He burst from the house, slamming the door so hard it didn't shut right."

"It didn't? You've got great eyesight," I commented neutrally.

"Yes, I do," he said stubbornly, daring me to disagree, which I didn't. "The man ran to his car and jumped in and slammed that door, too. It's a wonder the thing didn't fall off. Then he just took off without looking around at all."

"This is the guy who pulled out in front of me? The one who caused me to hit my brakes?"

Andy nodded.

I thought for a minute, fascinated by the idea of an angry man leaving Trudy's house on a night she was too sick to keep her appointments. Who was he and what was he doing there?

"Do you know who he was?" I asked Andy.

"Well, he had his collar turned up, and he was wearing one of those tweedy hats with the brim that turns down all the way around. On TV English guys wear them."

"Was he trying to hide?" I asked. "Or was he just trying to keep the sleet off?"

"Well, I've seen him around town other times, and I never saw him with a hat on before."

"So you think he was trying to hide."

Andy nodded. "He kept peering around, you know, like he was looking to see who might see him."

"But he didn't see you?"

"Not me. I hid behind a tree until he got in his car. Then I stepped between the cars where I was when you almost got me."

"Enough with the poor-me-you-almost-got-me bit," I said irritably.

Andy grinned unrepentantly.

"So you're saying you know who this guy was?" I asked.

"Yeah." And he stared at me, his feet kicking the air in a regular rhythm.

"What?" I said, because it was obvious he was waiting for me to say something. "You think I should know, too?"

Again I was back at Trudy's house, and again the car leaped at me with no warning. Again I felt cold all over, and again I hit the brakes.

I stared at the mental image of a man in a hat, collar up, as he flashed before me in the glow of my headlights. I felt tight with anticipation. Maybe now I'd get my zing of insight.

Seconds ticked by with only my stomach growling. I looked at Andy, shaking my head. "Nothing," I said.

"His picture's in the paper lots of times," he offered, as if he was giving me a clue.

And I knew. Just like that, I knew.

Andy grinned at me. "Surprised?"

I shook my head. "Not really."

"He's got money. He's not rich exactly, but he's not poor, at least not yet." And Andy laughed nastily.

"What do you mean?" I asked.

"Nothing."

"Andy, are you trying to get money out of him? Are you blackmailing him because he was at Trudy's that night? Is that why you're still around?"

Andy slid off the table and went to his laptop. "Wonderful little thing," he said, patting the machine. "And e-mail's the best of all."

"But why is he willing to pay?" I asked. "Just being at someone's house is hardly a legal offense."

"Yeah," Andy said. "But leaving the house in a fit of anger with a person lying dead on the floor is."

I stared at Andy until he began to squirm. "You

went into Trudy's house, didn't you?" I asked. "After I drove off."

"So what are you to make of it if I did? The door was open."

"What did you find?"

He cleared his throat. "She was already dead. She was lying on the floor in the bathroom in her night-gown, and she was already dead."

I shook my head. "The medical report says she didn't die right away."

He looked at me, his face lit by the gray wash from his laptop. "She was dead. She was. She was all white and dead. I know because I touched her, and she was cold."

"I'm sure she looked dead. The cold was shock, I would guess. But did you feel her pulse or anything?"

He shook his head. His face showed surprise and then, gradually, something else. Anger? "She *had* to be dead. She had to be. Do you really think I'd be dumb enough to let the one person who could have helped me die?" His voice shook with the unfairness of it all.

I thought this was a very good time to say nothing.

"But he *must* have killed her," Andy said. "At least involuntary manslaughter like me. Why else would he be willing to pay?"

"So you are blackmailing him."

Andy turned to his laptop and hit a few commands. Up popped a file. He invited me to read.

I saw you, you know. I saw you leave McGilpin's. And she's dead. How would that look to everyone? $10,000 and I won't tell.

"Andy! Don't you know this is against the law?"

"Do you honestly think I care?"

Good point. When you're wanted for killing someone, what's a spot of blackmail?

"So how did he respond?"

As Andy brought up the response, I heard a scraping noise outside his cubicle and what I could have sworn was a rapidly drawn breath. I got real still and strained to hear more, but there was nothing.

Andy again indicated that I should read.

I did nothing and you know it. Get off my back if you prize your position.

I stared at the last sentence. "What in the world does that mean?"

"I couldn't figure it out at first, either," said Andy. "So I wrote him again."

Like you can scare me. I can ruin your reputation, land you in jail, and you know it. $10,000 or else. By Saturday.

"And his answer?"

Back off, Merry. I don't like to play games.

"*Back off, Merry?*" I squeaked. "*Back off, Merry?* Where does that come from?"

Andy had the grace to look sheepish. "I didn't know he knew you."

"What?" I pushed him aside and began fiddling

with the laptop on my own. I called up the e-mail message about ruining reputations. There, large as life, was From: MERRY.

I rounded on him. "*From Merry?* Merry? My name? Whatever possessed you to send those vile messages in *my name?* How could you have done that to me?"

'I didn't know it was you!" he said, hands raised defensively. "I mean, I knew it was your trunk Pat was in, and I knew you were the one who almost hit me, but I didn't know *you.*"

"How?" I screamed. "How did you know Pat was in my trunk? How did you know it was me in that car?" I had never been so upset in my whole life.

"Your license plate," he said. "MERRY. When I dumped Pat, there was MERRY staring at me. And I didn't feel merry, let me tell you. When I watched you drive away after almost hitting me, there was MERRY again. I didn't even know *Merry* was a name. It could have meant happy or funny or something, like it belonged to a joker or a comedian. I didn't know you or anything. I certainly didn't know where you worked or lived or anything. I just needed a word to sign on with, and I didn't want to use *Witz.* He might know who that was or be able to figure it out. I needed a new account name. When I went to log on, 'Merry' popped into my mind because I'd just seen it a couple of times. But I didn't know he knew you! It's not like I was out to get you or anything."

I slumped against the worktable. "Oh, Andy." I wanted to cry at the absurdity of it all. "He thinks *I'm* the blackmailer. He thinks I'll tell people I saw him leave Trudy's. And Trudy died suspiciously, or at least without anyone seeing. That's why he's trying to kill me!"

NINETEEN

"You're right," a new voice said. "And I guess I should apologize, Merry."

Andy and I spun around. There he stood in the opening of the cubicle with a gun in his hand.

I felt the blood drain from my head, making me woozy. I grabbed the edge of Andy's workbench and held on. "How in the world…" I began

"You told!" Andy's face contorted with fury and he lunged at me.

"I did not!" I jumped behind the table for protection. "Tell him!"

Andy was too furious to hear me. "I asked you to come alone!"

"I did!" I yelled as I circled the table, Andy following. "I don't know how he got here."

"Yeah, yeah," said Andy as he surged up onto the table, preparing to leap on me. "Tell me another one."

"Back off, kid," yelled the intruder.

If Andy heard, he paid no attention.

"Remember, I warned you," the gunman said, and proceeded to fire his gun twice.

I jumped and screamed as Andy's laptop popped

and then died of its bullet wounds. Andy froze, then turned and stared in disbelief at his dead computer.

He now directed his wrath toward the man with the gun, a circumstance I heartily approved of. "Why, you—"

"Don't try anything!" The warning was sharp and cold. "I wouldn't mind shooting you, too. Or better yet, you move, and I'll shoot her." He shifted slightly and aimed his gun at me.

"Think I care?" Andy challenged, but he stayed on the table.

"Hey!" I scowled. "How come I'm suddenly expendable?"

But I was, and I realized it with the emotional equivalent of walking into a brick wall. I actually felt knocked backward, and all the breath was forced from my lungs. Now that I knew who had attempted to kill me, he couldn't let me go free. It would mean an arrest, a trial, jail and, most importantly to him, loss of reputation and position—if I ever got a chance to talk to anyone, that is.

I wondered whether Andy had yet realized that the man's being here with a gun sounded the death knell to his extortion scheme, too. Somehow, knowing Andy's unique thought processes, I doubted it.

"If she didn't tell you I was here," said Andy with a malevolent stare in my direction, "how did you know? What did you do? Follow her?"

"I read her e-mail."

I frowned. "How? It's a private file. You don't have my password."

"Whiskers," he said. "It wasn't too hard to figure out."

"Whiskers?" Andy repeated, still staring hostilely from his perch up on the worktable. If one of those people who say they can see auras were here, she'd probably see waves of black emanating from Andy, threatening, hating, plotting.

"My cat," I said. "My password."

Andy snorted. "How clever."

"What's yours?" I said defensively. "Welder?"

He didn't answer, and I knew I had hit it first try.

Instead he turned to the man. "You hacked into her private files?"

He nodded.

"You had no right!" Andy shouted. I wished I could believe he spoke because he believed in privacy and other constitutionally guaranteed rights, but I knew he was miffed because he had been found out.

"Look who's talking about rights," sneered the gunman. "The guy who smashed a wrench into an innocent man's head."

I don't think it was so much what the man said as the way he said it, but it was the last straw for Andy. He leaped.

I saw him dive, his arms and legs spread like some kind of giant, demented flying squirrel. His body seemed to hang in space forever before it plummeted down, a smothering weight.

As soon as Andy jumped, the gunman fired. Fortunately, in spite of what he'd said about shooting me, he turned the gun on the one jumping him.

And he missed, at least as far as I could tell as I ran out through the opening between the welding shields, out into the dark shadows of the main working area of

Brandywine Steel. I ducked behind the first big machine I came to as a second shot rang out, reverberating hollowly in the great building.

Andy screamed.

Dear God! I prayed as I tried to paste myself against the machine and make myself invisible. *Let him be okay!*

When I heard quiet, stalking footsteps, I knew the man was concentrating on me. That meant Andy wasn't going anyplace, at least for now. *Oh, Lord, please don't let it be permanently!*

"Merry," came his cajoling whisper. "Merry, where are you? I won't hurt you."

Right. And Jack's coming to marry me tomorrow.

I ducked as low as I could and fled to the next piece of equipment. I would have been fine if I hadn't slammed full speed into a workbench and jarred any number of things loose, including my teeth.

Through the ringing in my ears I heard him moving in my direction. I blinked back tears and struck off to the left.

"Come on, Merry," he said sweetly. "Why would I ever want to hurt you now that I know you weren't trying to blackmail me?"

And why would I ever want to let you know where I was as long as you have a gun in your hand?

I kept moving. It was a slow business because I was afraid of what I couldn't see. I came to an open space between two pieces of equipment. A security light far above showed dimly that there was nothing between the two pieces to bump into or fall over. I took a deep breath and dashed for the far cover.

My left foot hit the grease patch that lay silently, patiently waiting beside the far machine. My feet flew up. In the split second I hung suspended, I heard this "Oh-h-h-h!" that was unfortunately me. I twisted to keep from falling on my back, and that's how I slammed onto the concrete on my arm, my elbow taking much of the hit.

I automatically rolled into a ball, protecting my hurt arm, while I tried to breathe through the pain. I wanted nothing more than to lie there and cry, but I could hear footsteps racing in my direction.

Forcing myself to my feet, I slid behind the machine and hunkered down, still cradling my arm, forcing myself not to cry or sniffle or make any noise. If anything got me in trouble, it would be my hammering heart.

He thundered toward me and stopped on the other side of my hiding place.

"Come on, Merry. Let me help you," he coaxed. "You know I only want what's best for you."

I closed my eyes and shrank back into my machine. *Go away! Lord, make him go away!*

There was a noise from the other side of the room, and he turned toward it. A providential mouse? Andy? Who knew and who cared!

Thanks, Lord!

Slowly he began moving away from me. I made myself stay still until I was sure he was some distance off. Then I peered from my hiding spot.

I couldn't see him, but I saw the safe area where Andy and I had walked when we came in. If I could get over there, I could find the door! I could get away and get help for Andy.

Again I searched the darkness, but I couldn't see my pursuer, so I ran across the open area, watching for grease, workbenches and other traps. I had come to understand, in the short time I'd been stumbling through this darkness, that Andy's little lecture on safety was more than the ramblings of a misguided mind.

I was running down the safe area toward the door when the lights suddenly came on.

"Now I'll find you, Merry," my tormentor called.

I had felt fairly safe in my red coat when there was so little light. Now I felt like a neon sign. Blink, blink. Here's Merry.

I glanced back over my shoulder and saw him at the far end of the room. He saw me at the same time and began running in my direction. I felt a surge of adrenaline, and I knew I could make the door before he got near me.

Oh, Lord, don't let him shoot me!

I would have made that door if it hadn't been for the pallet that had bothered Andy because it was sticking out into the safe area. I ran into it going full speed, cracking my shin on a piece of the steel resting on it. Pain shot up my leg, and I fell forward, striking my head on a gas canister as I went down.

So much for escape.

When I woke up, I was in a dark, cramped place.

At first I didn't realize I was confined. I hurt too much to notice. My head ached, my elbow throbbed and my shin smarted. I lay with my eyes closed, trying to determine which pain was dominant, but it kept changing. Then I shifted my weight, and my elbow definitely took top honors as I rolled on it.

Hastily I changed position again and rested with my eyes closed for a bit longer. It was too much hard work to figure out where I was.

And then I remembered where I'd been, and my eyes flew open. Brandywine Steel! Andy! The gunman! I had to escape!

That's when I realized I was confined.

Groaning as much from déjà vu as pain, I realized that I was again in a trunk. But this time the car was moving.

All I could think was that my next car would be an SUV with no trunk—assuming I had the opportunity to *have* a next car.

The car I was riding in swerved abruptly one way, then just as abruptly the other. My elbow got another hefty crack, and I swallowed my cry. No sense letting the driver know I was conscious.

The engine died and the car shook as the driver climbed out. The front door slammed. I heard the driver walk past, gravel crunching underfoot.

I waited until I couldn't hear anything. Then I moved as quickly as I could. After my last stay in a trunk, I had vowed to never suffer the terror of entrapment again.

"You know, you probably don't have to, at least not in a car trunk," Sergeant Poole had told me. "Most cars these days have fold-down backseats so you can carry things like lumber or skis." It was obvious from his face which he thought the more important. I guess if I were a cop, the slopes would seem a fine refuge to me, too, even if I were overweight and grumpy.

I muddled around the back of the trunk, knowing that somewhere I should find a handle or a lever or a cord or something that I could pull to release the backseat. The need for speed made me fumble, but finally I felt the handle hanging down. I pulled on it with all my might and was rewarded with a faint click.

The backseat, released, opened slightly into the car under its own weight. At the same moment, I heard footsteps. I froze.

The footsteps slowed at the car, and someone bumped against the trunk. I listened with icy fear for a key to slide into the lock. Instead there was a bump on the side of the car, and a front door opened.

I wrapped my fingers around the edges of the backseat and tried to pull it back tightly against the trunk. I could see a halo of light around it and feel the whip of frigid air. I cringed. What if he saw the loosened seat? Or noticed my fingers? What if the seat fell forward under its own weight in spite of my attempts to hold it back?

Crouched in exquisite agony, I listened to him fumble and mutter. I was afraid to breathe for fear he'd hear me, for fear my breath would unbalance the seat beyond my ability to control it.

When the car door slammed and darkness returned, I slumped in relief. But when he stopped by the trunk, I tensed again. A key slid into the lock and my breath caught in my throat. I tried to remember what position I'd been in when I regained consciousness, but I hadn't the vaguest idea. Hopefully he didn't, either.

I let go of the teetering seat and tried to lie flat

without making a sound. I attempted to look limp even though I was strung as taut as a concert violin.

The air whipped across my face, and I wondered if an unconscious person reacted physically to something as uncomfortable as the cold. I had no idea, so I stayed still. I could feel him staring at me and struggled against the urge to twitch. After a seeming eternity, unable to deal any longer with the vulnerability of lying there blind, I slitted my eyes.

All I saw was a huge shape bent over the trunk, black against the black of the night. Every nightmare I'd ever had as a kid about the bad man who lived under my bed came flooding back. I was staring at evil personified.

Then my ogre sighed as if in great pain and slammed the trunk shut. I heard slow footfalls as he walked away.

I forced myself to count to fifty. Then I pushed against the seat and presto, change-o, I was free. The seat fell forward easily, and I slithered into the car itself. I was certain he was going to come back and grab me half-escaped, and I'd be back in big trouble. But he didn't return, and I scrambled out the door and into the fog.

When my foot hit the ground, my shin protested loudly and I almost fell. I grabbed the door handle to keep from falling and looked down. My shin was swollen to several times its normal size.

I touched the injured area carefully, only to find it wet and spongy.

"What in the…"

It was a scarf, carefully wrapped around my lower

leg, and it was wet with blood. *How kind of him to wrap my leg before he killed me,* I thought. *With any luck, I've bled all over his car in thanks.*

I was surprised to find myself in the parking lot behind *The News*. Why had he brought me here? Why hadn't he just shot me back at Brandywine Steel? Because he couldn't put a gun to an unconscious person's head? Because looking me in the face made it too hard? After all, he wasn't a professional killer or anything.

But I didn't hang around to ponder the riddle further. I limped to the police station as fast as my bleeding leg would allow.

Sergeant Poole was still on night duty, and more than efficient. In no time he had a stakeout in place behind *The News* and emergency vehicles on their way to Brandywine Steel to see about Andy.

He tried to make me to go the hospital to get my various injuries cared for.

"Don't waste your breath," I said. "If you think I'm going to miss the denouement of this story, you're crazy. I'm coming with you."

"Denouement, Merry?" he said. "Give me a break."

"Climax, peak, turning point, final action," I said.

"I know what it means," he said as he slapped on his bulletproof vest. "We cops are literate, too. I just don't know other people who use words like that in real conversation. Go to the hospital."

I just shook my head at him.

"It'll be dangerous, Merry," he said. "I think we have a very desperate man here, so who knows what he'll do. Possible gunshots. You might get hurt."

"I'm already hurt," I said. "And I promise to stay out of your way."

In the end, Sergeant Poole let me come along. His alternative was to put me in a holding cell until it was all over, and then I'd just write an article about how unfair he'd been.

"But you've got to wear this," he said, and handed me a bulletproof vest. I struggled to put the unwieldy thing on as I trailed him and several officers across the street.

"Remember, he's not in there alone," I called. "That's Don Eldredge's car—" and I pointed to a green Taurus "—and that's Mac Carnuccio's car." I pointed to a bright red Miata. "And he has a gun that he's already used."

In the end, Sergeant Poole and four other officers positioned themselves behind *The News.* Another officer watched the building's front door on Main Street, though no one expected our man to go that way.

"Are you going to go in?" I asked, breathing in the night's raw dampness as my heart fluttered in apprehension.

"No," Poole said. "We are not going in. That's how people get hurt. We wait."

I was placed behind a car not far from the sergeant as he crouched behind an unmarked police car issuing orders.

We had settled in for a long wait when suddenly, through the fog, came the whistled strains of "Merrily We Roll Along," and Curt came sauntering into view like Marshall Earp on his way to the OK Corral. Only he didn't know there was a showdown, and he'd left his six-shooters at home.

TWENTY

I looked frantically from Curt to the back door of *The News,* positive that our man was going to burst out at this very moment, guns blazing, and that Curt would get blown away in the crossfire.

I saw Sergeant Poole move to grab Curt and haul him out of harm's way, but I acted more quickly.

"Curt," I yelled. "Help. Over here."

He broke off whistling in the middle of the second "roll along." His head spun in my direction, and he leaped to my aid, just as I had known he would. As he got near me, leaning down to see what my problem was, I grabbed him by the coat collar and pulled.

"Stay down," I hissed in his ear as he thudded gracelessly to the ground. "You just walked into the middle of a police stakeout."

He pulled back and stared at me in disbelief, then scanned the area, taking in Sergeant Poole and the others. Sergeant Poole gave a little salute and signaled that Curt stay low.

"My stalker," I whispered. "We're going to get him."

"We're going to get him?" he repeated, looking

confused. He shook his head as if to clear it. "Why'd you call for help?"

"To get you out of the way. I didn't want you to get shot."

"You didn't?" He looked ridiculously pleased.

"I don't want anyone to get shot," I said primly, studying my hands.

He grinned. "Right. Now explain all this to me in a sensible manner that I can follow," he instructed. "What are they doing? What are you doing? What's going on?"

"Nothing special." I knew he was going to be mad when he heard the whole story. I would outrage all his protective tendencies and be unrepentant about doing so. "I just got put in a trunk again and I decided I was tired of it, so I got the police after him. And he shot Andy. And he tried to kill me those two times."

"Wait a minute, Merry. Just who are you talking about?"

I told him.

He looked at me with agitation and suspicion growing in his face. He zipped right past the information, even the identity of the stalker, and tackled me, as I had known he would. "When I left you this morning, you didn't know any of this."

"Right," I agreed. "I learned it all this evening."

"At your 'business meeting'?" He pronounced the last two words in verbal quote marks.

"Ah. You found my note," I said. "I didn't want you to worry."

"Which is undoubtedly why you worded it so blandly." He was so angry his voice shook.

"You're darn right, buddy," I said, tired of his righteous indignation. "I got a chance to meet with Andy, and you weren't going to keep me from going."

"Andy? Alone? Just you and him? You're crazy!"

"Maybe, but have I got a story!"

"Merry! What's wrong with you?" Curt hissed, grabbing me by the shoulders. "That's exactly what you promised me you wouldn't do!"

I looked him in the eye. "Oh, no. You *asked* me to promise, but I never did. I never would. I may be a coward in some areas, but never in the area of a story." I pushed his hands away.

"You can't go running around, risking your life like you were in a movie or something!"

"It's my life! I'll risk it if I want!"

"Oh, yeah. That's mature."

I scowled at him. The last thing I wanted to deal with was his sarcasm.

"Listen to me, Merry—" and up came his index finger "—you can't keep on like this! It's dangerous."

"And you can't keep telling me what to do!" I yelled, swatting at his finger, choosing to ignore the truth in his comment.

"Will you two shut up?" Sergeant Poole could barely get the words out through his gritted teeth. "In case you've forgotten, we're on a stakeout here."

I looked an apology, then turned back to Curt and whispered fiercely, "You can't tell me what to do!"

"Somebody's got to!" Curt spat, his finger right under my nose in the most infuriating, patronizing manner. He clamped his lips together and took several deep breaths. Then he repeated, suddenly gentle, his face pained, "Somebody's got to." His index finger lost its rigidity and slid softly down my cheek.

Dirty fighting, I thought as I closed my eyes to deal with my sudden vertigo.

"You've got a huge bruise, you know," he said.

"I do?" I lifted my hand to my cheek and rubbed. "No, I don't. It's only grease from when I fell and slid along the floor. Here. Smell." I held out my hand.

He took my hand and before I knew what was happening, pulled me into his arms. He nuzzled against my cheek and sniffed. "Um, you're right. Grease. A soft, feminine fragrance to please a discriminating man."

"Get away," I cried, pushing him back. "You're hurting my elbow."

"What's wrong with your elbow?"

"I cracked it when I fell and got the grease."

"Merry!" He reached out and took my elbow gently in his hands.

"Dr. Carlyle, I presume," I said snippily to cover the pain that flashed through me from fingertips to shoulder.

"It feels like a balloon!" He was horrified. "You've got to get to the hospital and get that treated."

I nodded. "Sometime soon."

"Merry!" He moved in close as if he wanted to slide an arm around my shoulders, probably preparatory to grabbing me and carrying me off whether I wanted to go or not.

"Be careful," I cautioned with a sweet smile. "You'll get blood on your clothes."

"Blood? Blood!" He stared, at a temporary loss for words.

"Blood," I said, and pointed to my wrapped shin. "I fell over a piece of steel when I was being chased. After he shot Andy. But he wrapped it in his scarf. Nice, huh? Wrap it up before you shoot her. Chivalry."

Curt reached to unwrap the wound and see what he could do about it. "Boy Scout," he said. "Lots of first-aid training."

"Don't," I said, putting a hand on his. "I don't want to know how bad it is until I can get it cared for."

He turned his hand over and grasped mine. Poor man. He was falling for me, and I was driving him crazy. Seemed only fair. His concern and affection were scaring me to death.

"Did you sell Mr. Harrison the picture?" I asked.

He nodded.

"For the full amount?"

He nodded again, and we sat side by side, hand in hand, leaning against a parked car, the fog seeping into our clothes, the damp ground slowly chilling our seats.

After a few minutes he said, "You're spunky." He paused. "I'm not sure I like spunky."

"I definitely don't like it," I said. "It rhymes with chunky and clunky."

He drew a line down the back of my hand with his thumb. "That's not what I meant."

"I know," I said gently.

"How about perky?" he offered after a bit.

I shook my head. "Rhymes with turkey."

"Feisty?"

"Feisty's nice. I like feisty."

He smiled lopsidedly. "I guess I'll have to learn to like it, too."

Good grief! An adaptable man! Now I was truly terrified.

More time passed while I wondered how many women held hands with men trying to like *feisty,* and all while they were on a police stakeout.

"Did he really shoot Andy?" Curt asked suddenly.

"You were listening!"

"Of course." He seemed surprised. "I always listen to you."

"Then why do you keep singing 'Merrily We Roll Along'?"

"Because I can't help it. I never knew anyone before who had whole songs written about her." And he smiled.

"You are ridiculous! And yes, he really shot Andy."

"How badly?"

"I don't know. I was running for my life. But the police sent emergency vehicles to help him."

Suddenly we heard Sergeant Poole's walkie-talkie squawk. I couldn't make out the words across the parking lot between us, but whatever was said energized him. He signaled one of his men, issued orders and began to climb into the car he'd been hiding behind.

I climbed over Curt and limped across the lot as fast as I could. "Where are you going?" I demanded.

"To Brandywine Steel. Andy's holed up there and keeps threatening to kill himself."

I grabbed the rear door handle. "I'm coming with you. He'll talk to me."

Sergeant Poole groaned, then nodded reluctantly. "You may be right."

I climbed in, only to be pushed forcefully from behind as Curt climbed in after me.

"Do you think I'm letting her go alone?" he said to the frowning sergeant.

The sergeant rolled his eyes. "I don't think she's alone, unless I count for nothing."

"I'm coming." Curt slammed the door behind him.

I studied Curt, torn as usual between irritation and delight that he felt I needed care. Noticing little droplets of mist on his dark ringlets, I stifled the renegade desire to brush them away before he caught cold.

It's hard to keep your seat in the back of a police car with a driver who is practicing all the fast-driving skills they ever taught him at the police academy and with no door handles or anything to grab on to. When we swirled into the lot at Brandywine Steel and screeched to a halt, Curt and I picked ourselves up off the floor and waited to be let out.

It took a knock on the window to remind Sergeant Poole to free us. As we climbed out, a cop ran up to the sergeant.

"It's not as bad as we thought," he said. "We think the kid's bluffing."

"Where is he?" Sergeant Poole asked.

"In a cupboard in the cubbyhole where he works."

"Why do you think he's bluffing?"

"We don't think he has a weapon."

"Do you know this?"

"No, we think this," the cop said. "We asked him to tell us about his gun, and he mumbled some things that you would only expect from a kid who's not really familiar with firearms. He messed up brand names and caliber and bullets and where he got the gun—everything. It sounds like more than just stress-induced confusion to us."

"You're probably right," I said. "When he killed Pat, he just used what was at hand, a wrench. And he didn't have a gun when I was here earlier."

Sergeant Poole grunted and looked thoughtful.

"Isn't he wounded?" I asked. "I thought he had been shot."

The officer nodded. "He's hurt, all right. We found him by following the trail of blood to this cupboard."

"Let me talk to him," I pleaded. "I've talked to him before, and I think I can get him to come out. Please?"

Sergeant Poole grunted again and thought some more. I watched him with a thudding heart.

In a matter of minutes, I was back in Andy's work area, though this time the B-movie atmosphere of impending doom was missing. All the lights were on, revealing the dirt and grime of an everyday workplace.

I swallowed the great surge of bile that rose when I saw the huge red stain on the concrete. Andy's blood.

"He's in there." One of the officers pointed to the bank of cupboards Andy had glanced toward when he told me he had been hiding here since the killing.

"Go ahead," Sergeant Poole told me, and I was conscious that everyone became silent and totally focused on me.

"Andy?" I said as I knelt in front of the dirty, once tan, now grimy-gray cupboard. I tried to keep my voice from shaking, to sound assured and comforting. "It's me."

"Merry?" A sob came on the end of my name.

"Andy, are you all right?"

"Help me," he whispered. "Don't let them get me."

"Oh, Andy." I glanced around at the officers, their guns either drawn or hanging on their hips, and at all the emergency medical personnel hanging back by the welding shields but watching intently. *Don't let them get me.* There was a piece of true Andy realism.

Andy groaned. "He shot me!" The shock and disbelief were audible even in his raspy whisper. "It's my shoulder. I never knew something could hurt this bad." And he sobbed again.

"Andy," I said, wishing I could see his face instead of just the cupboard door. "You need medical help."

"No," Andy begged. "Don't let them get me! Don't turn me in! I'll shoot myself!" He began to cry, and my heart twisted.

"Andy," I said with as much authority as I could muster, hoping I was right, "we both know you don't have a gun."

"How do you know that?" he asked. His voice was a whine, and I felt a surge of triumph. He sounded just like a young Sam used to when he made empty threats to his big sister, and I called his bluff.

"You've never had a gun. That's why you used the wrench."

He didn't argue the point, and I saw Sergeant Poole nod in relief, a few of his craggy worry wrinkles smoothing.

"Merry," Andy whispered conspiratorially, "I just need till Monday. My mom will get the money then, and I'll get the money from her and go away. No one will ever know I was here."

"I'm opening the door, Andy," I said. I reached for

the knob. "Don't be afraid. I just need to see you to be sure you're okay."

I slid the door to the side just a fraction and looked at his pale, terrified face, as colorless as the fog swirling outside. He was twisted into a small space in a corkscrew position that must have been uncomfortable even when his body was whole. Feeling overwhelmed by the foolishness and futility of all his choices, I reached out and touched his face. I started. "Andy, you have a fever! You need to go to the hospital!"

"No," he said pathetically. "I can't! They'll put me in jail."

"But you're sick. And you can't run your whole life."

"Yes, I can," he said pathetically as a great chill racked him. "I won't go to jail!"

I slid the door open farther and took his limp hand. "Come on, Andy. Give yourself up. You really have no choice."

Suddenly Sergeant Poole was beside me. "Thanks, Merry. We'll take over now."

When Andy heard the new voice, his hand, still in mine, convulsed.

"It'll be okay," I whispered to him, knowing it never would but not knowing what else to say.

"Yeah, sure," he said, totally defeated.

I stepped back, and Sergeant Poole moved in. He bent down, assessed the situation in a glance and signaled for the paramedics.

I stood with Curt, watching as they carefully levered Andy free. He screamed a couple of times as his injured arm was jostled in the process, and the sound pierced me. Curt slid his arm around me in comfort, and I leaned gratefully against him.

As the ambulance crew and the police carried Andy away, I thought I heard him say, "Oh, God, help me."

TWENTY-ONE

"**Y**ou need to go to the hospital, too." Sergeant Poole, his hand on his car door handle, looked sternly at me.

I shook my head. "Not yet. We're going back to the paper with you."

"Merry," he said in a combination of exasperation and resignation.

Curt and I piled into the backseat before he could argue further, and the sergeant drove sedately back to *The News*.

Our success with Andy had made Sergeant Poole talkative. "I'm glad you talked him out, Merry. And I'm glad he didn't have a gun to follow through on his threat to kill himself. There's nothing I hate more than suicides. People taking the quick way out, never thinking about the people they leave behind, the problems they cause for the moms and dads or spouses and kids. To me it's the epitome of selfishness. I hate dealing with it."

"A very final solution to temporary problems," I said. "Anyone who does it must be desperate."

"No excuse," the sergeant said as we pulled up behind the paper.

But suddenly I wasn't listening. Instead, my eyes were on the officers stationed on either side of the back stoop. I could see through the wispy fog that they were pressed flat against the building, their guns at the ready.

The sergeant saw them, too, and threw himself out of the car. As he hurried past, he grabbed our door handle and yanked it open. Then, crouching, he raced forward until he was behind the car closest to the building.

I looked at Curt and he at me. We hustled out of the car and ducked behind it. I had no desire to be closer. I just wanted to see what happened, not be involved in it.

Suddenly the back door of *The News* flew open and a man stepped out. Both officers jumped out from their positions against the building, yelling, "Freeze!" in a roar that would have frozen me.

It paralyzed the man emerging, stopping him with one foot on the stoop and the other poised over the top step. The officers rushed him, flinging him around to face the door.

"Assume the position!" they yelled as Sergeant Poole ran forward, followed by Curt and me.

Sergeant Poole was having trouble not laughing as he sputtered, "Wrong man, wrong man."

"Wrong man?" said a female officer whose name tag read Schumann. "Are you sure?"

"Wrong man," I said, enjoying the situation almost as much as the sergeant.

The erstwhile arresting officers stepped back sheepishly as Mac Carnuccio turned slowly around. He looked malevolently at Sergeant Poole. "I'll get you for this, William," he said.

"I don't doubt it," Sergeant Poole said with a happy smile, completely unintimidated by Mac's wrath. "But it'll be worth it, whatever you do. You were scared spitless."

"I was not!" Mac contested hotly.

"Yeah, yeah." Sergeant Poole was unconvinced. "Now tell me. Is Eldredge still in there?"

"Yeah," Mac said as he tried to understand what was going on. "He's writing away at his PC."

The sergeant nodded, pleased. "I just hope he didn't hear the yelling out here."

"Don is many things," said Mac, "but deaf isn't one of them."

"Are we going in after him?" asked Schumann. "He's in there alone now, isn't he?" She looked at Mac for confirmation.

"In after him?" Mac repeated.

Sergeant Poole shook his head. "Still too dangerous. We'll just wait out here. Positions, everyone."

"William!" Mac said, preparing to make a stand right there on the stoop until he had his answers.

"Long story, Mac. Just get out of the way! And fast!"

We all turned to go back to hiding when Mac noticed me for the first time. "Merry!" He started to follow me.

"This is my story, big guy," I said, just so there'd be no misunderstanding.

"Are you okay?" he asked as he ducked behind our car with Curt and me. "Don said he was worried about you. He seemed to think you'd been hurt."

"That part was right," Curt said with steel in his voice.

"Hey, William," Mac called across the open area between the rows of parked cars. "I hear you got the Gershowitz kid."

"Shut up, Mac!" I grabbed his arm while Sergeant Poole frantically signaled for silence.

"Cute hair," Mac said as he eyed my fog-wilted head. "And you've got grease on your face, beautiful."

I rolled my eyes. "You're incorrigible." Then what he'd said struck me. "What did you say?"

"Cute hair. You've got grease—"

"Not that. Before."

"Don's worried about you."

I shook my head wildly.

"They got Andy?"

I grabbed his arm again, this time in a vise. "How do you know that?"

"I heard it on the police band radio we have in the office. They said something like—" and he took on the tinny, squawky sound of the radio "—all units, stand down. Suspect under arrest and on way to hospital. Repeat, murder suspect caught and under restraint."

"You heard that? In the office? And Don heard it, too?"

Mac nodded, not understanding my agitation.

"What did Don say when he heard it?"

"'That's it. That's all there is, folks.'"

"He didn't say anything at all?"

"He said, 'That's it. That's all there is, folks.' Oh, and he also gave me his car keys and asked me to get something out of his trunk. 'Just put the keys under the floor mat when you're done,' he said. 'Be sure Merry's all right.' See? That's why I thought you were hurt."

I felt my blood congeal. "Sergeant Poole," I yelled, rushing from my hiding place. "He knows. Don knows you've got Andy. And he sent Mac to let me out of the trunk. And he said that it was all over!"

Sergeant Poole understood what I was saying. I could see the terrible possibility flood his face.

"I hate it!" he yelled as he pulled himself to his feet. We raced for the back stoop and pulled the door open.

"Don't do it!" the sergeant yelled just as the single, fatal shot tore the night.

I flinched as if I were the one who was shot and flattened myself against the wall to let the police charge past. I had no need to hurry, no desire to see what was awaiting us. Curt stood with me, but Mac rushed into the newsroom behind the police.

I heard Sergeant Poole bellow, "Don't anyone touch anything! Call for the crime-scene unit."

Squaring my shoulders, I took several deep breaths to keep from vomiting and stumbled to my desk. Curt pulled over Larry Schimmer's chair and sat with me, not looking much better than I.

I reached out for his hand. "I'm sorry," I said shakily. "I know this must be awful for you. Even though you were never close, he was your brother-in-law."

"It's probably no worse for me than for anyone else," he said, but the dark bruise of shock under his eyes showed differently. It's impossible to spend family occasions like Christmas and birthdays and funerals together without some ties, no matter how tenuous.

We sat in numbed silence as the crime-scene team

arrived and went about its business quietly and efficiently. Eventually, I took a deep breath and looked across the newsroom to Don's desk.

Don was slumped in his chair in front of the big picture window overlooking Main Street. His neat gray hair was missing from the back of his head, and tissue and blood spattered the wall, the floor, a large split-leaf philodendron and the reference volumes on the bookshelf behind his desk. For some foolish reason, the plant and reference books being stained really bothered me. I guess if you can't cope with large issues, you focus on small, insignificant ones.

The gun had fallen from Don's hand and lay on his desk next to his keyboard. The air smelled of explosives and death.

"At least it's indoors tonight," I said, and Curt nodded, understanding my reference.

After some time Officer Schumann walked toward us. "Merry, Sergeant Poole wants to talk with you."

I followed her across the room to where Sergeant Poole was ensconced at Mac's desk. I was glad to notice that Curt had followed me.

Sergeant Poole looked tired and edgy, his craggy face gray and more deeply furrowed than ever. "Why can't people be brave enough to gut it out and take responsibility for the messes they create?"

I glanced at Don and the body bag they were preparing for him, then looked away quickly. "I don't know."

The sergeant took a drink from the cup on the desk and made a face. "Cold."

"I'll get you a hot coffee, William," Curt said gently, taking the cup and going to the coffee machine.

"He wrote you a note," Sergeant Poole said to me.

For a split second I thought he meant Curt wrote me a note. Then I knew he meant Don. "Me?" My voice was a squeak.

"He left it on the computer. We printed several copies." He held out a sheet to me. "I hope it doesn't cause you more pain."

I took the single sheet like it would burn me. "I'll just take it back to my desk," I managed to force out.

He nodded.

It was several minutes before I could bring myself to look at Don's last words. Finally, with a huge sigh and a deep prayer, I read:

Merry:
I never meant for all this to happen. I hope you believe me.

When you came to work here, you were such a pleasure, my ray of sunshine to counter Mac's grouchiness. Trudy thought you were a cutie, too.

Then you told me you saw me the night Trudy died. And I got those threats. I couldn't believe you had turned on me. You! I told myself I was completely justified in attacking you. You deserved everything you got.

And it wasn't even you.

It's my temper. I've always struggled with it. When I came to Amhearst, I thought Faith Community Church would take care of it for me. That's probably also why I married Joan. She was so nice and kind and gentle.

She drove me crazy.

I know Curt thinks I abused her, but I only hurt her two times, at least physically. Unfortunately the consequences of the second time were tragic. But I didn't kill her. I just pushed her hard. I rushed out without even looking to see where she'd fallen. I didn't know she'd hit her head. I swear I didn't.

Talk about a guilty conscience. That's really why I can't stand Curt, you know. Just looking at him reminds me of what I did to Joan.

It kills me to think Trudy died from a head injury, too. If only I hadn't lost my temper and left her. If only I'd admitted how sick she was and how much she needed my help. If only, if only.

I never raised a hand to Trudy in anger though. She was more than willing to go toe-to-toe over an issue, but she would never have let me threaten her or hit her, and I knew it. She was too strong a woman.

I'm sorry about Andy Gershowitz. I hope he survives, though between you and me, he's a loser. And I'm glad you're okay. I just couldn't kill you, Merry Sunshine. I'm glad I failed before. Tonight, I just couldn't do it, especially when I'd lost the reason for my anger and self-justification. Of course, by that time I'd already dug my own grave.

Don't worry about me. I believe. At least I think I believe. I guess God'll tell me whether I've got it right or not, won't He?

Don

I was crying when Curt came to the desk, and I continued to cry as he read the note over my shoulder. I sniffed loudly and said, "At least you know what happened to Joan now."

"Or his version of it."

"Curt," I said, "he admitted manhandling her, pushing her. I think he was telling the truth. Why wouldn't he? He acknowledged everything else."

Curt sighed. "I've distrusted him too long."

I took his hand. "Things don't tie up easily in real life, do they? Believe him. For your own peace of mind."

He walked away, going to the coffee machine and pouring two mugs full. He stood there for a few minutes, and I knew he was struggling with some very deep and painful issues. I turned back to Don's letter.

I could tell Curt had returned when I smelled the coffee. I turned and took the mug he offered. The warmth of the mug made my fingers feel less brittle, and the hot liquid eased the chill in my heart.

"He said he believed," I said, nodding toward the letter. "I wonder what he meant. Did he believe in Jesus as his Savior?"

Curt shook his head and shrugged. "I don't know. I hope so. And I don't think the Bible says that killing yourself negates your salvation. It's wrong, just like lots of other things are wrong, but it doesn't cause God to ostracize you from heaven or anything."

I noticed Officer Schumann approaching us, and I tensed. What now?

"The sergeant says you two can go," she said.

"There's no more reason for you to hang around here tonight. He'll contact you when he needs you."

We nodded in relief and walked slowly to the door. I turned and looked back at the newsroom. It'd never be the same again. No Don sitting in ordered splendor before the great window, surrounded by Jolene's African violets. No Don handing out assignments or tearing into substandard writing. No Don saying, "Charge it to *The News.*" My eyes filmed with tears, and I had to swallow several times to get rid of the lump that threatened to choke me.

One sign of normalcy stood out in the room like a beacon. In the middle of all the police activity sat Mac, hunkered down at Edie's desk, typing like crazy. I knew what he was doing.

"He's writing an article for Monday's paper," I said. "Do we even have a paper to print anymore? What happens when the owner/editor kills himself?"

Mac must have felt our eyes on him. He looked up, saw us in the doorway and came hurrying over. He was crackling with tension and energy.

"Merry, I need your copy on your conversation with Gershowitz and your capture and escape from Don."

"Mac!" I was stunned, though I'm not certain why. If he was working as usual, of course he expected me to do the same. "You don't have to do it tonight," he said magnanimously. "You can come in tomorrow or wait until Monday morning, but I need that material by the deadline. We're going to assume we have a newspaper until someone tells us we don't, and we've got a major story to publish!"

"She won't be in next week," Curt said. "Can't you

see she's emotionally spent? She needs some time off."

"She'll be in," said Mac, looking at me dispassionately. "She's a newspaperwoman." And he turned back to his desk.

I nodded and kept nodding as I walked outside. I was too tired and drained to think much right now, but I knew Mac was right. We still had a paper to produce until someone told us otherwise, and I was a writer for that paper. Maybe tomorrow I could put some words together, maybe not until Monday, but I would do it.

Curt drove me to the hospital where we waited while the emergency personnel dealt with a teenage girl who had unsuccessfully slit her wrists and the girl's mother who kept crying, "Why? Why? What did I do wrong?"

Next a young couple came running in with a baby who was having trouble breathing. Then came the ambulance with the victims of a car wreck and a man with a profusely bleeding head injury. He sat in a chair near us as he waited to be seen, a huge towel held to his head.

"She didn't mean to hurt me," he told us. "She was just mad, and the frying pan was the closest thing."

We nodded our understanding as a young woman took her seat next to him and grabbed his hand.

"I didn't mean to hurt you so bad," she said, tears ruining her mascara. "I was just so angry at you, and the fry pan was right there!"

"See?" he said to us. "I told you."

The result of all this activity was that Curt and I had lots of time to talk before anyone got around to a woman with a swollen elbow and a badly cut shin.

"Don and I both came to Amhearst looking for something," I said as I settled into the curve of Curt's arm where it ran across the back of my chair. "What happened for him? How did it turn out this way?"

Curt shook his head. "A series of bad choices, I guess."

"But why didn't any of us see it coming?" I asked.

"See what coming?" Curt rubbed at the grease on my cheek, succeeding only in getting it all over his fingers. "His uncontrollable rages? His need to protect himself and his position at any cost?"

"But friends should see trouble coming and stop it," I said. "I feel we failed him."

"Friends probably should," Curt agreed. "But we were hardly friends in any deep way."

I knew he was right, but I brushed his comment aside as too easy. "Maybe if Trudy hadn't died, things would have been different for him. I think he really loved her."

"Maybe it would have been different," Curt said as he rubbed the grease from his fingers onto his jeans. "But she did die—and maybe she died because of his temper, just as Joan did. He has made horrendously bad, even evil, decisions for years, decisions that almost cost you your life, too."

I waved my hand as if the attempts to kill me were just so many misunderstandings.

Curt took my hand. "Merry, look at me. What I have to say is important."

I turned to him. *Such a fine face and such honest eyes,* I thought.

"You can't explain everything, and you can't fix everything," he said seriously. "Life just isn't that neat."

I stared at him for a minute. "Didn't I just say the same thing to you in reference to Joan's death?"

"Did you?" He looked surprised.

I nodded. "Back at the paper."

"Oh," he said as he scrambled to remember. "Then you're very wise."

"Right. And I can see that you really do listen to me." But I smiled.

He smiled, too, as he stared at the grease residue on his hand. "There's not a day that goes by when I don't berate myself for not seeing how serious things were for Joan and not helping her somehow. But I can't change anything no matter how much I want to. I can't go back. I just have to learn to live with what is."

"Guilt and regret," I said as I reached out and rubbed the grease on his hand. "They'll get you every time, won't they? I guess part of learning to press on is learning to deal with them."

"And the only way to deal with them is to put them in the arms of God every time they threaten you." He closed his hand around mine. "Believe me, I know."

We were silent for a few minutes. If no one else showed up bleeding all over the place, I should be next for treatment.

"One more thing," Curt said. "Wrong is always wrong. Don't get all soppy about Don now that he's dead. He still tried to kill you. He still pushed Joan. He still shot Andy Gershowitz."

"Marshmallow Merry," I said as my name was called. "Always feeling sorry for the guy in trouble."

Curt gave my hand a brief squeeze. "Caring about

people is a wonderful thing," he said. "Just keep it in perspective."

It didn't take long for me to get a tetanus shot, an ice pack for my elbow and a sturdy dressing over the stitches in my shin. Curt would have to stop at a convenience store for a new supply of Tylenol for me on our way home, and he could take me to Brandywine Steel for my car tomorrow. I didn't have the stamina to get it tonight.

My mind was so occupied with thoughts of the night's events that I didn't even notice the lilac tree when we finally walked to my door. Real horrors had pushed imaginary ones aside.

TWENTY-TWO

Curt and I went to the hospital Sunday after church to visit Andy.

"Are you family?" the receptionist asked us suspiciously.

When we reluctantly admitted that we weren't, she said, "He's in critical care and under police guard. No visitors but family."

Knowing his mother's plans, I thought we'd be a safer bet than she, but I recognized a closed door when I saw it.

"Will he be all right?" I asked.

She consulted her computer. "He's doing as well as can be expected."

"Thanks," Curt said, and I think we both were thinking *for nothing*.

"Sergeant Poole can get us in," I told Curt with more confidence than I felt. "We'll call him tomorrow."

When we got back to my apartment, Curt walked me to the door.

"I've got to take a nap," I said. "Last night I kept waking up every time I fell asleep, either hearing a gunshot or seeing Don or rolling on my elbow. Maybe today I'll do better. I need to. I've got to get some rest so I can write my story."

"Oh, Merry." Curt, who looked so fine in his denim shirt, sleeves rolled up his forearms, was distressed. "Don't let Mac pressure you. Don't write that story. You don't have to."

"Sure I do. It's my job. I can write here on my laptop and send it in electronically."

"But it's not good for you to keep reliving it." He followed me in when I opened my door. "Just relax and let it all go."

"I find writing helps me deal with things," I said. "It's cathartic."

"I think you should just take some time off. I really do. It's pretty rough, what you've been through."

I shrugged as I hung up my coat, noticing that Whiskers had shed all over it and I hadn't even noticed. What was it about white cat hair and navy-blue wool?

As much as I wanted to, I didn't offer Curt a hanger.

I turned to him and saw Whiskers's hair on his navy Dockers. Maybe I should get the animal shaved like a poodle, with the little tufts at ankles and head. Maybe that would solve the shedding problem.

"I learned some important things through all this," I said to Curt as I picked absently at the white hairs on his shirtfront. "I learned that pressing on is making choices, hopefully good ones, and learning to live with the consequences. And I learned that it takes character and guts to make good and godly choices."

He nodded. "Sounds right to me." He grasped my hand and pressed it against his chest.

I pulled my hand back, turned him around and pushed him toward the door. "Thanks for being there several times when I needed you," I said to his back so that I didn't have to deal with his melting brown eyes. I resisted the urge to de-Whiskers his broad shoulders. "I don't know what I would have done without you."

He grinned, obviously pleased, as he looked back over his shoulder at me. "I think you know that I like being there for you."

"I've gotten that idea," I agreed. "Now you've got to go. I'm going to sleep, then work."

He spun around and stood facing me. He took a step closer, and I took a step back. He pretended not to notice. "Take your nap. I'll go take one, too. Then I'll pick you up and we'll get dinner and—"

"No, Curt. I have to write my story." I felt like yelling, *Turn on your hearing aid, you handsome idiot!*

"Merry," Curt said, and his index finger came up to help him make whatever point he wanted to make. I didn't give him a chance.

"Curt!" I stood legs apart, hands on hips, in a typically attractive feminine pose. "Don't tell me what to do! I mean it! Stop trying to manage my life! You're a wonderful guy in a number of ways, but hasn't anyone ever told you you're bossy?"

I yelled the last endearment over the ringing of my cell phone.

I grabbed my purse, fumbled for my phone, flipped it open and barked, in the same sweet, dulcet tones, "Yes!"

"Hasn't anyone ever told you you're stubborn?" Curt said stiffly.

"Feisty," I corrected him, and ignored his "Ha!"

"Merry, babe," came a voice over the phone. "You were right. I was wrong."

"Feisty-schmeisty," said Curt. "Obstinate is more like it. Independent to a fault."

"*Whose* fault?" I snarled. "Not mine."

"That's right," said the happy voice on the phone. "That's what I said. Not yours. Mine."

I held the phone out and stared at it. I jammed it back against my ear just as Curt stuck his nose inches from mine and said, "Sometimes I wonder if you're worth the emotional upkeep."

Glaring at Curt and unexpectedly cut by his words, I yelled into the phone, "Who *is* this?"

"But then I think about it," Curt said with a sweet smile, "and I know you are."

My knees nearly buckled.

"It's Jack, sweetheart," came the happy voice down the miles. "I miss you, and I want us to get married in June. How about the fifteenth?"

This time my knees did buckle.

Dear Reader,

If you have read *Caught in the Middle,* you are an answer to prayer. How's that for an unexpected and wonderful thing?

Several years ago when the Caught books (*Caught in the Middle,* April 2007, *Caught in the Act,* May 2007, and *Caught in a Bind,* June 2007) were first printed, I asked the Lord for certain sales.

To my sorrow the books did not do that well. I was very disappointed because I love Merry. I thought she had a lot to share with her readers. I continued to ask for that sales number, though I couldn't imagine how that prayer could ever be answered.

Then the books were declared out of print. Now I really couldn't imagine how that prayer could be answered.

But God heard and He has answered through the joy of seeing these three books reprinted by Steeple Hill Books. I have even been given the joy of writing a fourth Merry book, *Caught Redhanded,* August 2007.

The moral of this story? God answers our prayers in His time and His way. I thank you for being part of this truth in my life. What surprising answers or unexpected timing have you experienced? Share with me at gayle@gayleroper.com or at www.gayleroper.com.

Gayle

QUESTIONS FOR DISCUSSION

1. Merry takes a huge step when she leaves home and moves to Amhearst to save herself. Have you ever had to take such a huge step? Or maybe a small one? How did that work out?

2. Her work in journalism has honed Merry's problem-solving skills, enabling her to solve the mystery. How have jobs you've held honed your talents in unexpected ways?

3. The theme verse for this book is Psalms 32:8. What part of this verse is the most comforting to you? Why?

4. Merry forces herself to go to the bell choir. What benefits come to her for taking that risk? What risks have you taken that have paid off for you?

5. Patrick's fiancée Hannah holds herself responsible for his death. What are your thoughts about this issue? What about when you are really responsible for someone's hurt? What do you do with the regret? What are three steps the apostle Paul gives to help us deal with regret in Philipians 3:13–14?

6. Patrick's mother, sister and nephews suffer from his death. What are five practical things that can be done to help people who are cut to the quick like they are? Are there people in your life who could use this kind of TLC?

7. Andy Gershowitz is briefly suspected of being Patrick's killer as a result of a romance gone sour. Have crimes of passion happened in your community? What can you, as a Christian, do to minister to those affected?

8. What led Don to the place he could take his life? Was his suicide the act of a strong person or a weak one? Why?

9. Much of *Caught in the Middle* has to do with choices and the consequences. Read Joshua 24:15. Long, long ago Joshua leveled this challenge at his people. How does this challenge apply today? How can it safeguard us in our choices?

10. Name five ways in which Jack and Curt differ. Which suitor should Merry pick and why?

REQUEST YOUR FREE BOOKS!
2 FREE RIVETING INSPIRATIONAL NOVELS PLUS 2 FREE MYSTERY GIFTS

Love Inspired®
SUSPENSE

YES! Please send me 2 FREE Love Inspired® Suspense novels and my 2 FREE mystery gifts. After receiving them, if I don't wish to receive any more books, I can return the shipping statement marked "cancel." If I don't cancel, I will receive 4 brand-new novels every month and be billed just $3.99 per book in the U.S. or $4.74 per book in Canada, plus 25¢ shipping and handling per book and applicable taxes, if any*. That's a savings of 20% off the cover price! I understand that accepting the 2 free books and gifts places me under no obligation to buy anything. I can always return a shipment and cancel at any time. Even if I never buy another book from Steeple Hill, the two free books and gifts are mine to keep forever.

123 IDN EL5H 323 IDN ELQH

Name	(PLEASE PRINT)	
Address		Apt. #
City	State/Prov.	Zip/Postal Code

Signature (if under 18, a parent or guardian must sign)

Order online at www.LoveInspiredSuspense.com

Or mail to Steeple Hill Reader Service™:

IN U.S.A.: P.O. Box 1867, Buffalo, NY 14240-1867
IN CANADA: P.O. Box 609, Fort Erie, Ontario L2A 5X3

Not valid to current Love Inspired Suspense subscribers.

Want to try two free books from another series?
Call 1-800-873-8635 or visit www.morefreebooks.com

* Terms and prices subject to change without notice. NY residents add applicable sales tax. Canadian residents will be charged applicable provincial taxes and GST. This offer is limited to one order per household. All orders subject to approval. Credit or debit balances in a customer's account(s) may be offset by any other outstanding balance owed by or to the customer. Please allow 4 to 6 weeks for delivery.

Your Privacy: Steeple Hill is committed to protecting your privacy. Our Privacy Policy is available online at www.eHarlequin.com or upon request from the Reader Service. From time to time we make our lists of customers available to reputable firms who may have a product or service of interest to you. If you would prefer we not share your name and address, please check here. ☐

LISUS07

Love Inspired SUSPENSE

TITLES AVAILABLE NEXT MONTH

Don't miss these four stories in May